Praise for Thon

Seasons & Days

"*Seasons & Days* reads like a dream of the natural world, and that is not surprising because Thomas McIntyre is closer to his game than any writer ever."

Terry McDonell
Editor, *Sports Illustrated*

"Tom McIntyre can make you laugh and learn in a single sentence. He is undoubtedly the most thoughtful—and thought provoking—outdoor writer we have today."

Jameson Parker
Author of *An Accidental Cowboy*

Dreaming the Lion

"There is a certain temptation to term him our finest living hunting writer…"

John Hewitt
Gray's Sporting Journal

"McIntyre is at once storyteller, poet, and magician in a well-crafted work that confirms him as one of the icons of field literature…[He] is a thinking man's outdoorsman, a true philosopher who can be read for pure entertainment or, like Nabokov, read for the exhilaration of seeing what a guy with a real grip on the writer's craft can do with philosophy and fun."

Clive Siegel
Game Trails

The Way of the Hunter

"Tom McIntyre's...portrayal of the compassionate human predator expresses the true sentiments of the legitimate outdoorsman, be he a hunter or fisherman."

Peter Hathaway Capstick

Days Afield

"As literate and informative an outdoor writer as one is likely to discover..."

American Library Association's Booklist

"...the naturalist hunters' new poet laureate."

Stephen J. Bodio
Author of *Querencia*

"Hemingway without the hubris."

Robert F. Jones
Author of *Blood Sport*

"Sheer, unapologetic masculinity is perfectly balanced by magnificently crafted writing.

David Graber
The Los Angeles Times

The
SNOW LEOPARD'S TALE

Published in the United States by

Bangtail Press
P. O. Box 11262
Bozeman, MT 59719
www.bangtailpress.com

Cover paintings and interior illustrations
by Joel Ostlind

The
SNOW LEOPARD'S TALE

by

THOMAS MCINTYRE

Illustrations by Joel Ostlind

BBangtail
Press

Montana
2012

...MAN LIVES IN TIME, in successiveness, while the magical animal lives in the present, in the eternity of the instant.

Jorge Luis Borges

VIENS, mon beau chat, sur mon cœur amoureux;
    Retiens les griffes de ta patte,
Et laisse-moi plonger dans tes beaux yeux,
    Mêlés de métal et d'agate.

Charles Baudelaire

Where the mountain peaks ended in the sky, Xue Bao parted three eyelids. The third, red-stitched membrane floated off corneas clear as bright pools of water. Outside the hollow where he lay curled under overhanging dry gray stones, the sun rose smoke orange, shaded by the dust whorled by the wind of winter's end. As his head lolled between loose front paws, Xue Bao watched the morning light sweep toward him. The raw air carried the sharp bark of a marmot, and he listened on, his nose distinguishing scents. After a time he unwound his body and on his side stretched heavy-muscled legs, spanning his toes, claws revealed like petals opening. Rising to his paws, he swayed his back, yawned eburnean fangs, shook down from neck to thrust hind right leg, flicked his tail, and strode from beneath the rock shelf on Bountiful Black Mountain into the sunrise that spilled across the east in the rufous tint of sand-fox fur.

Xue Bao traversed rocky pitches. The mountain's naked crests screened the silhouette of his body and long tail. He moved almost invisible in the dawn but was substance surpassing shadow.

He was large for his kind, powerful-shouldered, deep-chested, his gripping paws large for his body and fringed in fur that let him travel atop the crusted snow of north-facing slopes. Thickened pads protected his paws from the knapped blades of fissured rock, while remaining sensitive to the inscription of the smallest spall.

He was longer than the tallest man was tall, half that length a black-tipped tail so furred two hands could not circle it. He carried his tail low; and when he moved in a low-bellied glide it brushed behind like the stroke of a plume.

Xue Bao had a short face, pink nose, small ears, white chin. Long vibrissae bristled translucent from whisker pads, an old furless scar chasing the broad bridge of his muzzle. He called in a wordless voice, never a roar.

Xue Bao's finest beauty next to ensnaring eyes the milk blue of tomb jade was his hide. His fur was amber-and-gray brume that clung to him. Large black rosettes floated in the fog, the patterns various, clouding into immaculate belly and chest, all of it kept washed by his tongue. No other fur was as warm and dense, and biting winds never passed through to prickle his flesh.

When he hunted in this fur, Xue Bao sheathed his claws until he pounced, then brought them out like mica hooks. The long ivory canines splintered bone and locked strangling holds on vulnerable throats, serrated side teeth shearing through hide. With claw and fang he brought down animals many times larger than he. Made intemperate by hunger he once leapt onto the longhaired humped neck of a wild yak; but the bellowing bull tossed its broad horned head, wheeling Xue Bao high in an arc through the air. Righting himself before the ground, Xue Bao landed heavy on his paws, crouching stunned, glaring at the bull, then ran, making no ventures toward full-grown wild yaks after that.

Xue Bao was born in the spring high on Bountiful Black Mountain in a stone den lined with the fur of his mother's coat. His mother, biting the scruffs of their necks, carried a twin and him from lair to lair and laid them down to sleep silent and secreted while she hunted, waking them when she returned, rasping her tongue on an ear and touching her nose to theirs, bearing the scent of new blood. She lay, and Xue Bao whined and found her milk, flexing his toes against her white belly, his brother suckling and mewing beside.

From his mother, his brother and he learned to hunt. In imitation they pantomimed concealment, slinking, stalking, succumbing between to the temptation of clumsy bouts of tumbling sham combat. They made first kills, springing from crags, catching and holding with claws, breaking fragile cervical bones with canines, suffocating with clenching jaws. Then one morning the brother was an immobile ball of matted fur at the base of an eroded loess bluff. As Xue Bao watched, his mother raked the earth-powdered corpse from a slip of xanthous soil, smelled it, abandoned it. His mother and he hunted on.

In time his mother was transformed. They rubbed faces and the next day she sissed when he drew close. Her tail lashed as she rotated her ears, the white spots on their backs presented to him. She lunged, cuffing at him with her paw, not letting him lie beside her any longer or share her kill. Driven out, Xue Bao became a nomad appropriating shade and night, wandering until he found his own part of the mountain, driving off an aged male leopard who could not fight to hold it.

Bountiful Black Mountain etched upon him its wind, snow, glaciers, chines, ravines, caves, ledges, paw-wide trails, and animals. He spent his waking hours rounding his near-vertical reach of it, his life an encompassing of the mountain.

Along narrow trails he scuffed to dark sandy soil with his hind paws and marked the spot. He found his own scent under beetling rocks; and rampant, he rubbed the sides of his face against the scented places. He dropped and turned, lifting his long tail stiff, jetting the rock with pulsed opalescent streams. If the scent of another male lingered on a rock, Xue Bao tracked him and drove him away. If the scent were a female's, Xue Bao sought her on the echoing of her call.

On the mountain, crepuscular Xue Bao hunted from first light to midmorning and from the end of day to late into night. He hunted big animals and small, finding enough, killing only the one he needed. Sometimes an animal (never a grown yak) was too large to eat whole, even over several days; but golden-feathered eagles, sail-winged griffons, and obsidian-pennated black choughs came down to scavenge what was left behind, able to feed because Xue Bao's teeth opened hides too thick for their beaks to pierce.

On Bountiful Black Mountain dwelt sheep, colored a mix of blue, gray, and brown, with short white legs, white bellies, blue-black chests and faces, and rock-smoothed olive horns turning out and back. A band could number sixty with sixty noses, sixty sets of ears, sixty pairs of eyes, sixty networks of triggering nerves for Xue Bao to hunt among. It took an hour, as sunlight traveled on a cragged face, for him to steal a hundred feet, hunkering in shade, and plunge down the cliff after one blue sheep, only to have another see him before he leaped, putting the band to flight. Or at the end of a headlong rush Xue Bao pounced and missed or had the sheep tear from his claws sunk in its flanks before he could close his jaws on its throat. For all that the hunting was never so testing that the mountain did not give him what he needed, Xue Bao squandering nothing during his ringing of it.

Then one late-winter morning when he was five, Xue Bao fell upon a band of wild sheep digging with the hard rims of their cloven hooves for tuberous roots on the warm south face of a cliff above a deep gorge. He came down on the back of a sickle-horned ram, driving it to the ground and the air from its lungs with a loud expiration. Xue Bao's teeth cracked the ram's neck, disarticulating vertebrae, severing the spinal cord, the sheep's sudden paralyzed weight launching Xue Bao down the cliff, haunches first, pebble stones sifting beneath them. Jaws clamped, Xue Bao fought against the skid into the gorge. Clinging to the ram's body, he braced his hind paws and dug the claws of his front into the cliff, the scratching tips scoring the stones.

The remainder of the band bounded back and forth, seeking escape. A ewe sprang below Xue Bao. Its lamb of the season leaped after the ewe, trying to stay close. It landed on a rock that clattered from under it, empty air below. The ram's lifeless bulk caught on an outcrop, and Xue Bao pulled himself onto the dead sheep, watching the lamb fall, cryless, solemn.

The band fragmented. For minutes Xue Bao only breathed. Then he cut into the stiff-haired hide with carnassial teeth. He crouched atop the ram, riving, swallowing, his jade eyes open, looking. Steam wisped from the ram's flesh; muscle fibers twitched as last sparks of electric current fired through dying nerves. Xue Bao ate, tearing off great bites until the meat cooled, blood incensing his fur, maddering the white of his chin.

Belly full, Xue Bao had to drink. He switched down the cliff, tail swinging, into the gorge and found water seeping from a crevice. He lapped the trickle running over algal-green stone. When the blood thirst was slaked, Xue Bao, feeling too heavy to climb back, walked, soft pawed, up the gorge. He came upon the lamb on the ground, shattered but its hide intact. The birds that scavenged by sight would not find it, deep in the umbra cast by the cliffs, not even to peck the soft iridescent eyes. Instead of carrying the carcass back to the ram's and staying by them for the days it took to eat it all, sated Xue Bao walked on until he found his faint scent from some past time in a gap under leaning blocks of stone. He slipped in, turned once on the cold rock floor, and slept into the night and through the next day.

Awakening in lowering darkness, Xue Bao did not go back to the dead sheep even then. He hunted for a new kill, better, fresher meat. He prowled the mountain for blue sheep where he had always found them, now finding none. On the third day he went back to the carcasses, hungry for even rotting scraps. All he found of the ram was stripped ribs and crushed bones, surrounded by coarse foreign scents and toed tracks, large but narrower than Xue Bao's pugmarks and punctuated by the indents of claws, overprinting one another. Below in the gorge something had discovered the lamb and carried it off, leaving the same alien spoor.

Xue Bao saw no more wild sheep, alive or dead. Marmots halted their barking. He hunted pika, but there were none. Xue Bao had known hunger often; but after eight days, his fat and flesh were wasting, his hide caparisoning his skeleton, numbered ribs waxing beneath it.

On the ninth morning griffons quartered the salmon-washed sky. Xue Bao surmounted a ridge and stood, the sun behind. Below in a patch of snow stood a dark large swept-horned ram, being killed.

Three wolves marked the points of a constellation. Two were gray near-grown cubs with black hackles on their scapulas and spines. The third, the she wolf, was redder on her head and forequarters. Wolves came from low country. Xue Bao had never scented but only seen them before at distances where their dog's eyes were not strong enough to see him, but now these had climbed above their range to hunt animals that inhabited his black mountain.

One of the wolf cubs sprang side to side before the ram, dipping its head as if in sport, which it was for it. The sheep was larger than any one of the wolves and held its head down, scything its horns

to keep the cub off its throat and muzzle, its braced hooves embedded in the snow. The she wolf and the other cub darted in as the ram kicked, their shown incisors snapping at the white patch of its rump. They closed their jaws on the ram. It took time, but the she wolf began pulling wet viscera from the sheep. The ram bleated, staggered, collapsed, lifting its open-mouthed head and letting it fall soundless. The second cub came to the back, crouched beside the other two wolves, and fed with them. Tufts of soft fur wafted. Red tinctured the snow.

Xue Bao stepped off the ridge and walked toward the wolves, round paws padding loose and heavy, head down and held forward, tail curled at the tip. One of the wolflings lifted its long-snouted head and stopped eating. It stood, then the other. The she wolf stood, silent, regarding.

Their ears were up and their mouths closed as they roved out in a line. They looked past Xue Bao, studying the air beyond and without him. One wolfling shot its eyes toward Xue Bao who held the cub's gaze until it turned its head sideward and took a hesitant step in retreat, hackles rising in involuntary response. But Xue Bao could not make them all back away; and they were flanking and probing toward him, mouths open, when Xue Bao knew the sheep was theirs.

He turned uphill, swiveling his head to watch the wolves trailing like cloud shadow over the bare slope. After a short way they stopped and went back to the sheep. As Xue Bao crossed the ridge, the griffons sideslipped out of their gyres, landing beside the carcass with a hop. The wolves returned; and as they lay down again around the ram, the large birds waddled away in distress, holding their wide wings up as if repelled by contact with earth and snow.

After that there were no blue sheep or the flesh and bones of any other animals, dead or alive. The next day, the only sound audible to Xue Bao his muted pant, he came to a ridge that ran off the mountain. His head felt almost too immense for his gaunt body, weighing on his bowed neck. He looked down the ridge, then back at the mountain's summit. In either direction lay silence. He took a step into the silence, heading down.

Xue Bao walked on slopes and cliffs and through defiles he had never before surveyed, moving to lower country, not sleeping in the day, not finding even faint scents of wild animals here. The inertia of descending slopes carried him on, drawing him off Bountiful Black Mountain without his looking back.

With large-pawed steps he descended the mountain's lower hills. Late in the day he was too fatigued to keep on and sought shelter in a rock-strewn wash. He found none with his smell, or any smell similar, but discovered a cave with thin slate tablets tilted against the rock outside its entrance. White-green lines like claw marks scored the tablets, and on one was the figure of one of the big dogs that accompanied the herders into the mountains in summer. Inside the cave were heaped large charred bones.

Xue Bao saw disarticulated tibia and fibula, together as long as his own tail, the broken wings of the pelvic girdle broad as a carrion crow's span, coop of ribs high as his own shoulder, a huge skull, domed, sutured, flat faced and unsnouted, the teeth ebonied and worn and gapped in their arcade in the jaws–even the best were too blunt for hunting and none large and square enough for profitable grazing–all sunk into blackened taphonomic process. Xue Bao recoiled from the pile, curling in the farthest corner of the cave, wrapping his long tail around his muzzle, eyes blinking closed in time, sleep finding him at last.

The slightest sound always woke Xue Bao; but he heard nothing as he lay unconscious through the night, inhaling the osseous air of the cave, his body twitching and his jade eyes ticking behind closed tripartite lids. Ropy saliva hung from his mouth and his lips parted over long yellow-white canines. His large paws swiped the cave floor, as if he hunted in his sleep. Or sought a means of escape. What he dreamed he would not remember. He never recollected dreams, or knew upon waking that he dreamed at all.

Late in the morning he awoke not from the buoyant black emptiness that had always been his sleep but in an oppressive exhaustion as if he'd been in desperate flight from a place of peril. He slunk from the cave, pressing against the side of the opening, keeping his distance from the bones.

Xue Bao flinched as the ocher sunlight of this foreign country struck his eyes outside the cave. Blinking, he set off, journeying through the day, stealing between coverts, watching, listening, scenting, slowed by apprehension. He had not covered a great distance before it grew dark, so he walked and hunted on through to daybreak.

At dawn he saw a compound of earthen-colored buildings on the small bare flats below. He crept to a ledge and looked down, ears flattened, only his jade eyes showing. The buildings were mud brick, enclosed by a wall the height to which a standing man could reach and lay a final course of sun-dried blocks. In the dirt yard three tamed yaks were gathered. Their coats of long shaggy fur, brushing the ground, were patched in white (the coats of true wild yaks solid black). Frayed ropes cinched crossed pieces of wood, smoothed by wear, to their backs, other frayed ropes bridled their muzzles and heads. Xue Bao recalled their size, and his body remembered the sensation of wheeling through air. After that he didn't look at them anymore.

Poles with colored cloths beating like wings in the wind were planted around the yard. Spindled on rods in a recess in a wall was a row of large yellow hammered metal canisters bright as standing flames

13

in the dusty sun. A woman with a saffron hide and a head of short black fur appeared and walked to the canisters, turning them with the flat of her hand and setting them spinning. They whirled and flashed, and when the woman finished at one end, she went back to the other so that all the canisters spun at once. Across the yard another woman with short black fur on her head and a saffron hide around her shoulders scuttled dried yak dung from a large mound into a battered gray metal container with a handle and carried it through a low dark doorway, lifting her black-slippered foot over a raised threshold, then reappearing with the container, emptied, to gather more dung from the heap.

Xue Bao watched for a long time, the pupils of his jade eyes shrunk to black singularities, searching for a way to stalk the women. He never saw humans as prey before, but now they looked easier for killing than yaks.

He saw no concealed route that would let him reach either of the women and pounce, and what would be the way to kill them? Like a sheep? Where to bite on such short necks? In a while he heard small bells chiming in the distance. Two straight-shouldered stocky ponies, one gray, one chestnut, with long unshorn rippling black manes, trotted toward the walled buildings. Men mounted on the bouncing backs of the pigeon-breasted animals had long sticks of metal and wood slanted across their backs. Pressing his belly to the ground, Xue Bao slid back from the ledge and into a wash, following it to a place of cleft rock where he hid and slept through the day.

When Xue Bao awoke, unrested, and went out from the cleft, scattered clouds crossed the moon. Traveling through shrouded foothills, he passed more man-tall mud-brick walls. He smelled dung smoke and saw lights, small and twinkling as stars, over the walls. Ponies and sheep (different from blue sheep—these with fleece white and curled) were penned, nickering and baaing. He kept his distance from the enormous black-and-brown dogs chained around the herders' houses. The dogs, larger than wolves, had fierce eyes sunk into folds of black hide, white spots in the fur above; and as far as Xue Bao kept from the walls, they caught his scent, their alarmed barking like the sounding of yellow-metal night gongs warning him to come no nearer.

He passed herds of long-furred, tamed yaks, bedded on the open ground. They scented him and rose from hind legs, heavy brass bells clapping, butting witless calves into the center of the fold, nervous even after Xue Bao moved far from sight and smell in the darkness. When he passed a second herd of yaks that night, Xue Bao was no longer in the narrow confines of canyons or on rolling foothills but had come out on the smooth sandy ground of a plateau, widening the gap between him and Bountiful Black Mountain with each soft step.

Dirty snow patched the plateau. The wind blew

harder than on the mountain and in its foothills. Xue Bao found the shank of a long-dead wild ass with black dried sinew on the bone but could not bring himself to try to eat it. Farther from the mountain than he had ever been, he continued from it nonetheless, looking for better hunting ahead.

At first light Xue Bao saw tiny, black-horned, tan-and-white gazelles springing through the cropped grass and snow. He stalked them in full daylight without cover. Over and over he slunk on his belly for hundreds of yards. He pressed himself tight as a snow bank to the ground; but when he raised his eyes the gazelles were always farther off, their slender-legged, slanted, united running like the skimming and shifting of birds in flocked flight over the gazelle-colored plateau. The last time he raised his eyes the gazelles dissolved in a shimmer of reflected radiation in the frozen air, their rumps flagging flashes of white. Xue Bao raised himself from the ground, all his strength spent. He looked for canyons in which he could trap gazelles or ledges from which he could leap upon them, but saw none. This was prey for the lowland wolves that did not hunt alone but ran in packs.

On the treeless plain the one elevated place was a wind-sculpted sandstone tor. Pulling himself up the loose dirt on its side, Xue Bao climbed to the level top twenty feet above the ground, finding a spot that was not spattered with eagle and griffon chalk. No wild animal would walk beneath for him to pounce onto; but it was at least a place where Xue Bao could try to sleep through the day, unseen from below. Curling around himself with his tail around his muzzle he closed jade eyes.

That day Xue Bao ran in his sleep without rest through a dream he would not remember. He woke past dark, the moon a drumhead sailing across the vault of the sky. Xue Bao sat, watching the moon, wearier than when he first lay down. As he watched, the orb's upper edge began to dissolve.

The moon's light was erased into the dark. Xue Bao was more transfixed than afraid. After a time the moon was gone. Only a faded ember, the color of the sand fox's red crown, rested on the black shingle of the sky that sparkled with burning stars. As if released from thrall, Xue Bao lowered his head and looked across the plateau.

Under the starlight the black shape of a pony approached, walking from the direction of the wind. Xue Bao saw that it would pass beneath the sandstone tor. He'd forgotten his hunger during the moon's leaving the night; but now it returned, filling his belly and head with a feeling of flame and ice.

The pony neared, and Xue Bao hunched his body, gathering what strength he had left in the muscles of his hind quarters.

A HERDER SAT A PONY, warm beneath a fleece-lined hat and wrapped in a high-collared fleece-lined chuba with sleeves that fell over his sun-and-wind-darkened hands. Until an hour before he had been smoking tobacco, drinking barley wine, and singing songs to a plucked lute in the lantern-lit warmth of the black yak-felt tent of his uncle, another herder, and now as he rode back to his own tent and sleeping wife, his eyes had grown heavy-lidded. He sat in a saddle with a high pommel and higher cantle, the bare wood of the tree padded by a red-and-white wool blanket thrown across it. The stirrups were gray metal, polished by the leather soles of the rider's black boots, each stirrup tied on by a rawhide thong.

The herder bent forward, nodding in and out of sleep. The braided rope reins ran between the fingers of his hand on the pommel, buried in the sleeve, while the other sleeved hand lay on the crest of the pony's short, dusty-maned neck. The pony found the way; and the herder, as sleeping people do, dreamed.

The herder's dream was a recurring winter one, of summer sunlight on the water of the lake called Teal Sea and the sheen of his wife's black hair as she made yak butter tea on a fire beside the round wool tent and his red-cheeked children laughing in play, his dream flocks growing fat and fleecy on the green grass and white-cupped flowers carpeting the land. It was a dream he was meant to remember when he woke, humans recalling dreams, if only in fragments and remnants.

Scenting only the pony and not the man, and seeing four hoofed legs, Xue Bao tensed, his muscles knotting like water-saturated cords. He raised his belly off the chalk-spattered sandstone. He leaped.

The pony's nostrils flared as Xue Bao's form blotted the stars from the black sky above. Teeth showing to the snaffle, the pony reared and screamed. Xue Bao stretched longer. The herder jerked up with half-closed eyes.

The pony came down, crouching on its front legs, spinning away, its shod hooves scalloping out soil as it galloped, a red-and-white blanket flying from the bare wooden tree of the saddle.

A PALE-ORANGE MOON arced westward in the blue-black sky, a last penumbra scudding from its full face. Xue Bao woke with his face pressed on sandy ground. As his eyes opened, fear clutched him. He stiffened, then in the next instant tried to jump to his four paws and run. Instead, he rose in unaccustomed segments to two hind paws and stood, tottering. In the dark he heard the sudden snort and frightened whinnying of a horse a hundred yards away, then the sound of its galloping off. Now he was alone.

The fear ebbed and Xue Bao scanned his surroundings, a tor looming over a plateau marled by dusty moonlight, trying to comprehend a perspective from two legs. He bent his neck and saw his hind paws. They were covered not in spotted fur but in scraped black shiny skin reaching almost to his knees. There was no fur above the knees, just a slack hide. A heavier hide hung down almost to his knees, covering his upper body and back, cinched by a wide band of skin circling his waist. The hide dangled down over each of his forepaws, concealing them. Xue Bao shook his paws above his head to slip the hide back. These paws, too, were furless, the padded toes elongated, retracted honed claws now broad blackened nails appearing unsatisfactory for the capture of anything.

Xue Bao brushed the grains of sand from his muzzle with the tips of the toes of his strange new forepaws. Where bristled whiskers and fur had grown he now felt thin hairs on an otherwise smooth chin and upper lip. Sliding his toes upward over his flattened face, he found more hairs above his eyes; but the rest of his face was as furless as his new paws. There was a heavy hide, like that over his upper body, covering his head; but when he touched it, it shifted. Wondering and frightened, he raised both paws and lifted off the hide, waiting to feel ripping and blood. But there was none.

His hand grazed stubble on the top of his head as he brushed across it. He held the hide from his head in front of him and saw that it had fur on the inside, and there were long flaps to cover his glabrous ears. He placed the hide back on his head, holding it with his paws for a time to ensure it would not dislodge by itself. He looked at the hide covering his upper body and saw that it had its fur on the inside, too, the fur of the herders' sheep. Xue Bao took his paws from his head and felt the curled fur inside the hide, running his tongue over his teeth as he did. His fangs, once long, were short and blunted, his mouth sour. His scent was now dung smoke and dried sweat, not the tended mountain wildness of his hide.

Under the moon Xue Bao's paw fell onto the wide band of skin around his waist. Cold metal-and-horn hung in a holder of carved horn. Xue Bao had always needed his teeth or both forepaws to hold anything. Now he closed one paw around the metal-and-horn and drew it from its holder. The horn end was carved, with figures in white metal on it. A pointed rigid tongue of metal grew from the horn, catching the moon. He turned it in the light, blinking as it flared at him. He touched his own tongue to it, shivering at its feel and the instant shallow incision it performed, the metallic of blood added to the taste of metal. Its edge would cut yak hide clean. As Xue Bao bent to slip it back into its holder he looked behind. There was no tail. He turned twice; but his tail was gone, along with his own fur, his own fangs, his own claws.

Xue Bao looked from his vanished tail back toward the mountain, but it was too distant to make out anymore. Hunger smoldered in his belly, and he turned in the direction he had been traveling since he began his descent. Anurous, he swayed, trying to take an upright step on two legs. He lurched and his right leg shot forward and caught him. He leaned again, and his left leg went out. Stumbling ahead, two legs now more liable to tangle than four, he had to walk almost a mile before he stopped focusing on his legs and found a stride.

Daylight came soon after Xue Bao began walking. He kept on, careless about being seen, though he did not know why. Needing to make urine, he scraped with his heeled hind paw, not feeling the ground as he would with his naked pads. He searched around on himself but couldn't see from where urine was made. After more examination, and discovering that he could uncinch the band around his waist and unwrap the hide from around his body, he saw where. With some disquiet he made urine in the scrape and scuffed soil over it.

He had a thin covering hanging over his chest and belly, and before he wrapped himself back up, he lifted it to look. Under everything, his body had spare patches of fur, and his ribs and hipbones jutted beneath naked skin. To Xue Bao it looked like a flayed hare. He remembered crouching in the rocks and watching the herders when they came onto the mountain, and he understood that their hides came on and off as they wished. Without them they must be like he, now, so it was good they did not shed their hides often.

Cinching the band back around his waist, he walked on until sunset. For the first time Xue Bao felt alarm in the deepening darkness that he'd always welcomed before. He sought a sheltered place to sleep and found only the base of a tall pole set in a pile of rocks, half a dozen taut ropes tethering it, the ropes and the pole hung with hundreds of tattered gossamer pieces of colored cloth snapping in the wind. Wrapped in his inside-out hide that was not as warm as his spotted fur, Xue Bao made an awkward backward sitting, like a stack of twigs toppling, and curled up.

He listened to the cloth snapping and the wind singing in the guys through the night. At first light he uncurled from his rocky bed, made a few drops of urine without making a scrape, and walked on. His dry throat and wounded tongue scratched, but he had been without food for so long that the hunger was growing numb. He climbed a small rise at the edge of the plateau and crossed through a pass between high hills, drifted snow, specked with yellow-orange dust, lingering in the shadows. Standing in the pass he looked at the land rolling out below, plotted in angled sections.

Something came into Xue Bao's head. Before, he had known—when to hide, when to run, when to kill—nothing more needed. Now he looked at the sectioned ground and saw more: something about the way the land lay, had been laid out, forming something in his head he turned over and put down in a place where he could come back and pick it up again. With this disturbing perception gathering within, Xue Bao walked out of the pass and started down a steep ravine, leaving the plateau behind.

The wind that swept the plateau clean of snow slackened. Xue Bao sank into banks deeper than the tops of the naked skin of his new hind paws, but he did not feel the cold touching him. He scooped up a clump of snow and sucked the moisture from it, a frigid bolt piercing his skull.

Dark rocks thrust out of the snow of the ravine, muddy paths tracked by the hooves of tamed yaks along the sides. Halfway down a trail, Xue Bao walked up on a herd of many-colored yaks. Only a few lifted their heads as they walked, lowing, bells clapping, and did no more than glance at him as he pressed through them. Beyond the yaks Xue Bao passed a round black wool tent, its sides oiled by the hides of the yaks and sheep that pressed against it in the cold weather, pitched on the side of the ravine. A herder in a hide like his came out. Xue Bao almost ran, but the herder raised his empty forepaw. Xue Bao stared but did not lift his own in return and kept walking, turning his head forward again. At the bottom of the ravine was a wide dirt trail.

The trail curved back on itself and back again then ran straight onto leveling ground toward buildings ahead. It brought Xue Bao to two rows of one-story earthen-colored buildings, addressing one another on opposite sides of the trail. A scarf of yellow-gray smoke was drawn over the building tops. The smoke did not smell like burning dung but something harsher. Xue Bao's nostrils quivered and itched, his eyes watered, the back of his throat stung.

In the smoke Xue Bao smelled scorching meat. He walked down the center of the trail to the building from which the smell came, the aching returned to his stomach. A lard pig, its skin the color of the bottom of Xue Bao's new forepaw, snuffled up the trail, snout to the ground. When it was still yards away it raised its small-eyed head and snorted. Unlike the tame yaks on the trail the pig made a loud squeal and wheeled, running with short jiggling steps and flopping ears into a narrow gap of packed earth between two buildings. Xue Bao held back from giving chase. He walked on.

Xue Bao stopped at a building with a large wheeled machine in front. A heavy-padded deep-blue hide hung over the building's opening, the smell of the meat rolling from behind it. Xue Bao poked the hide with his forepaw to see if it were alive. Then he drew it aside and walked in.

A man stood in front of a fire coming from a hole in a broad flat rock, shaking a big blackened metal pan with a long handle over the flame. A woman stood beside him, turning a bent handle that made a wind roar through the fire that shot up in white blasts from the hole. The fire had the same harsh odor as the smoke in the air outside. On the stone floor beside the broad rock was a dented metal bucket filled with glistening black rocks. The man lifted the pan, and the woman used wooden tongs to pick up a black rock and drop it into the hole. As fire flared, Xue Bao heard a sound in the pan like rain spattering on hard ground. Scorched-meat smell came from the pan.

The man and woman shouted when Xue Bao entered, bowing to him. The people did not startle Xue Bao but the shouting did. Then he understood that they were not shouting at him in anger but calling to him. He saw that the hides on the man and woman were different from his, not as thick and without any fur, buttoned to their throats, nothing covering their heads except straight black hair that grew there. White disks were set on the flat rock around the metal pan; piled on them were large pieces of smoking meat. Xue Bao stepped forward, reaching toward the meat with his forepaw (which at that moment he recognized as a hand; its toes, fingers; the black rocks, coal; the disks, plates; everything now particular). The man and woman shouted again, but this time there was anger in the sound. Xue Bao's hand halted.

He stared at the meat. The man and woman shouted more, their faces rigid, two straight lines between their eyes. Xue Bao now understood things but was without words to speak them—perhaps without a voice. The man went on shaking the pan and the woman cranking the handle as they shouted. Xue Bao lifted his head. He met their eyes, and they went silent.

The woman ducked her head. She looked at the floor, then turned her eyes up at Xue Bao, making soft sounds. The man raised a slow hand and with a small bow gestured toward the adjoining room. Xue Bao turned and walked into it.

It had been warm in the first room, near the flames; but it was warmer in here, a metal box on the floor glowing dull red, as if containing its own particle of the sun.

Another man sat in the room at a small table many-times coated with chipped white paint. Behind him, set in the wall, a square sheet of translucent ice let in clouded light. The man's hide was light-blue and all one piece. In front of him on the table were plates and bowls and a column of colored liquid— holding itself in the air and steaming like fresh-killed meat. The man with the light-blue hide lifted the column of liquid to his lips and drank. In the other hand, held between fingers, was a smoldering white stick. He put the end that did not smolder to his lips and inhaled, making the other end glow like the metal box. Lowering the stick, he exhaled two jets of pallid-gray smoke from his nostrils.

Xue Bao was watching the man to see if he would breathe smoke again when the woman came in carrying a silver-colored tray with white bowls and plates on it. She made more soft sounds and nodded her head toward another small table with chipped white paint across the room from the blue-hide man. Xue Bao went there.

He stood beside the table. Looking back at the blue-hide man, he saw how he was bent up on joined pieces of wood, like the joined wood set in front of Xue Bao's table. Xue Bao bent his body and lowered it onto the pieces of wood in front of the table.

The woman set down dishes from the silver-colored tray, then stood back, shielding herself behind it. Xue Bao looked at the bowls and plates. One had large chunks of meat in brown juices thick as blood. Saliva seeped into the corners of his lips. He lowered his mouth to the plate and took the meat in his teeth.

The meat seared Xue Bao's lips. He dropped it and sat up. Curling his upper lip, he showed pink-gummed long white teeth, and hissed. The woman shrank back. Across the room the blue-hide man, pouring steaming liquid from a pot into the column, looked at Xue Bao and went on pouring until the liquid ran out over the top of the column and spilled onto the table and onto the man and he shouted.

Xue Bao paid no attention and sniffed the dropped meat which was like none he'd ever smelled before. He stared at it, not knowing how to pick it up again. The woman watched. Still holding the tray in front of her, she approached him.

The woman took two wooden sticks from a cup filled with sticks on Xue Bao's table. While Xue Bao watched she mimicked picking up a piece of meat from his plate with the pinched ends of the sticks

Thomas McIntyre

and holding it near her lips and blowing. She nodded at Xue Bao, making little circles in the air with the sticks, her full lips pursed. Xue Bao looked back at the meat on the plate, blew on a piece of it, and when it cooled picked it up with his black-nailed fingers and placed it in his mouth. Even cooled the meat was warmer than any Xue Bao had ever eaten from the freshest kill, the flavor not like anything from the mountain.

The hot food made him warm, and he opened his chuba and shrugged his arms out of its sleeves and rolled it down around his waist. He ate until there was no meat left then bent forward and licked the juices from the plate.

After mopping the plate with his tongue he slid it aside and looked at another one on the table, with green plants limp and steaming. Xue Bao drew it to him and blew on the plants as the woman had shown, lowering his head at first to feed the way he would on plants on the mountain when it was mating time, then picking the plants off the plate with his fingers. There was a bowl of small white things like white ants heaped together. He picked up a sticky clump and put it in his mouth. He finished the bowl and wiped it out with his fingers then licked off the white ants that stuck to his fingers. When the woman had placed the plates on the table she poured for Xue Bao from a long-spouted kettle a column of liquid like the one the blue-hide man had. Now it was cooled and he bent forward to lap it. It was bitter but wet.

Thirsty, Xue Bao lapped the liquid until it was too low for his tongue to reach. He looked at the blue-hide man who was looking sideways at Xue Bao. The blue-hide man lifted his column to his lips and tilted it back. Using both hands Xue Bao tipped the liquid from his column into his mouth, some of it running over his chin. He put down the column, and the woman came with the long-spouted kettle and filled it again. Xue Bao let the liquid cool and using just one hand drank it down. He did this four times until his belly was full then sat back and swabbed his hands with strokes of his tongue, rubbing the wet backs over his mouth and face.

Xue Bao saw the woman, standing stiff, holding the kettle by the handle, the man from the other room beside her, holding something long and blunt-ended along his leg, the blue-hide man now staring straight at him. Xue Bao stared back. They looked away, the man and the woman backing into the other room and the blue-hide man fixing on his hot drink. Xue Bao lowered his licked hands to his lap.

Xue Bao's left hind paw itched. He rubbed it with his other black furless paw, but the itch would not go away. He remembered how his paws hadn't felt the touch of the snow, but now under the hide this one itched. Xue Bao rubbed his paw against the wooden leg of the table, but the itch persisted.

The heel of Xue Bao's paw caught on the table leg. He pulled back his leg and felt his paw's black hide slip. He felt no pain but was tense as he kept sloughing the naked black hide from his paw. At first he was afraid to see the paw with the hide gone, but after a few moments he moved his head and looked under the table.

Beneath his paw's black hide was short fur of many colors. He studied it, then drew up the hind paw and crossed it over his knee. Where the hide came up on his ankle, Xue Bao slid a finger into the top and husked off the fur.

Stripped, the paw was ashy, long, calloused, and tortuous; and like his fingers, the claws were gone from the toes, replaced by the half moons of nails with torn ends. The paw had bumps and knobs, and the soles were soiled, never licked. It was a foot.

Xue Bao looked at it and the corners of his mouth tugged up. Something rose in him, out of his belly. He laughed at the foot. Xue Bao's laugh was loud panting breaths. It felt good, as did his scratching the itch with ragged fingernails.

The blue-hide man was staring again. Xue Bao stopped laughing and pulled the many-colored fur—a sock—and the black hide—a boot—back over the foot, covering the curious specimen. The blue-hide man looked away. He finished breathing in the last of a stick of smoke and stubbed the end into his empty plate, then stood and picked up a silver bottle, worn through to patches of dull gray, and pushed a red rubber stopper into it. Reaching into his pocket, he placed colored paper and bright metal on the table. He crossed the smooth stone floor into the fire room, carrying the silver bottle under his arm, glancing back at Xue Bao as he went. As he vanished around the doorway, a brief angle of light flashed a man-shaped shadow on the cobbles. The couple, blinking as if awakening, shouted after the blue-hide man, bowing as he left.

Slipping his arms into the fleece-lined sleeves, Xue Bao drew the chuba up from his waist around himself. He slid his licked hand into a slit in the side of the coat and felt a pocket and some paper and metal. He took it out. The pieces of paper were wrinkled winter leaves with stolid faces drawn on them. The metal was stamped with numerals and letters Xue Bao could not decipher. He spilled them out, the paper fluttering, the metal clanging, onto the table. He stood and followed the blue-hide man out of the rooms, not turning his head as he passed the man and woman who stood back, close together, neither bowing nor making a sound, the woman shielding still behind the large tray and the man still holding the long handle with the blunt end.

On the trail that ran between the earthen-colored buildings, the blue-hide man stood beside the large machine with black tires shaded orange with road dust. Its long-hooped back was covered in a green tarpaulin, tied down with ropes. Xue Bao studied it until the man, who had been looking at something under the machine, turned and saw him.

After a second the man spoke to Xue Bao. Xue

Bao stared. The man turned away, walking to the rear of the machine—a truck. He started to walk around it, then stopped and looked at Xue Bao again. He came back.

The man spoke once more. He stepped past him toward the front of the truck when Xue Bao still did not speak. Xue Bao followed him with his eyes. The man pointed, then reached up and pulled open the side of the truck, gesturing inside.

Walking to the opening, Xue Bao saw two sitting places inside. In front of one was a black wheel, not as large and fat as those under the machine. The sitting places were as high as his head, the floor coming to his chest.

Xue Bao looked back toward the mountain, unable to see it through the yellow smoke and dusty haze.

Flexing his knees, Xue Bao was in the truck in a single spring, on the seat without the wheel. He sat with his hands on his knees, eyes ahead. A sheet of ice, like the one in the wall of the eating place, but transparent, hung in front of him, stopping the wind. Xue Bao leaned forward and touched it with the tip of his tongue. It was solid but not frozen; it didn't melt when his tongue touched it. He sat back, looking through ice that was not ice, while the blue-hide man went on holding open the side, motionless, his eyes on motionless Xue Bao.

The man roused himself and closed the side of the truck and disappeared. From the mirror over the windshield hung a long-tasseled knotted red string with a cluster of four small bright-painted masks; and held by two bands of rubber to the visor over the black wheel was a hazy picture of a standing woman, the corners of the photograph dogged. A few seconds later the man opened the other side of the truck, hoisting himself up into the driver's seat, looking at Xue Bao as he did. As he closed the truck door he ran his hand down the tassel of the red knotted string with the small masks without looking at it; and then he reached forward and turned something and the truck made a grinding sound, then began to growl. Xue Bao stiffened. The man rattled a stick in the floor, metal grinding. The growl grew louder, and the truck jumped forward.

The truck bounced hard, creaking as it rolled down the dirt trail with the rows of earthen-colored one-story buildings on either side, then passed under a red gate. Gold dragons and white symbols were carved in the wood across the top of the gate. Xue Bao couldn't read them but knew the symbols were writing and that the gathering of buildings they were leaving was a village. Beyond the gate the trail went from dirt to broad smooth unbroken black rock, and the truck rolled on faster with fewer bounces. They had to slow almost to a stop when a flock of white sheep blocked the trail. Two women in chubas with red wrappers around their heads and faces so only their eyes showed, herded the flock. When the sheep had flowed around it, the truck rolled on again.

The blue-hide man smoked and talked as Xue Bao stared silent through the windshield at the trail, which Xue Bao knew now was a road. Sand rose and lashed across the road, turning the air red yellow, abrading the outside of the machine. Xue Bao could see only a few feet ahead. The driver decelerated to a speed slower than when they drove through the flock of sheep.

Other trucks and cars came out of the blowing sand on the opposite side of the road. Motorcycles passed with riders doubled on them, black goggles over the drivers' eyes, the ones behind without goggles holding their eyes shut and their heads tucked down. All the vehicles crawled.

For an hour they traveled through a sand cloud. Then the road curved down, toward lower land. The wind and sand lifted, and it grew colder. Since leaving the ravine and village there had been no snow. Now as they followed the road down, the sky grayed and flakes fell.

The blue-hide man worked the stick, and the truck's growling grew louder and higher pitched. The road coiled like a serpent slithering over a rock. Xue Bao saw it far down the slope where at the bottom it turned once more and passed through a group of mud-brick houses with tall weathered double wood doors and closed wooden shutters, the houses squeezed against one another, not scattered as in the foothills or on the plateau below the mountain. Across the road from the houses was a field of mute gray stones lined equal distances apart, each stone cauled with snow.

The road proceeded through canyons and down slopes, passing under other gates, past more houses and walls and gray stone fields. They traveled lower and the fabric of the sky went on unfolding in darkening tones of slate. Wet snow still fell, vanishing as it settled on the wet ground. In a deep canyon the trail followed a river that ran over rocks and foamed white, steps of edge ice climbing the banks.

Across the river, men in buttoned black jackets and flat caps worked on the side of the canyon with mauls and iron bars and wedges, cleaving ten-foot tablets of granite. They did not raise their eyes from the granite as they struck it, white chips of stone splintering.

A shrieking came from high on the wall of the canyon, louder than that of any animal Xue Bao knew; but none of the men lifted their heads. Something long, coupled, black-green with yellow bands along its flanks, shiny scales scintillant, flew across a cut on the canyon wall, howling, breathing dense smoke. Xue Bao watched, trying not to be afraid. He looked at the blue-hide man from the corner of his eye; but the blue-hide man paid no heed.

Train. And Xue Bao quieted. That is what he

recognized, without having the word. As with truck and driver. White sticks, cigarettes. Colored liquid, tea. The sitting place a seat and joined wood a chair. The long-handled blunt-ended thing in the cooking man's hand, a weapon. All unsaid identities.

Now the road rolled out before them as it exited the canyon. They came to another gate, this one larger and more ornate than any other they had traveled through. Past it, Xue Bao saw birches standing in measured rows like snowcapped stones, lining either side of the road. Here were more trees than Xue Bao had ever seen, taller than any rock spire on the mountain. He craned forward, staring up through the windshield at their leafless branched tops against the leaden overcast.

More snow and rain came. Along the road walked people in thick dark coats, their hands behind their backs. Others rode bicycles, the men in caps, the women with knit scarves wound around their noses and mouths, red cheeks and deep-black hair, sprinkled with flakes, showing above the scarves.

The road was wide before they came to the gate, then narrowed past it; and the bare trees went away. Ahead Xue Bao saw buildings pressed close together, none made from mud bricks. Some rose higher than the height of five birches and seemed to be all glass, the glass dingy and streaked even in the cold rain. Others were made from small fired bricks or large concrete blocks. They had flat roofs, many with copses of metal towers sprouting on them. There were old buildings painted red. Their high roofs of curved glazed red tiles seemed to hover over them; and down the sloping, upturned rooflines ran rows of small ceramic stone lions, phoenices, qilins—green or blue—four, five, six in a row, the line topped by the open-mouthed fishtailed chiwen, talisman against fires. Only a few buildings were old; but even the newest looked antiquated, sooty, and dull, as if unable to be cleansed of the grime of the air.

They drove farther and the buildings grew taller and concrete sidewalks appeared. More people crowded onto the sidewalks. The buildings loomed like featureless cliff faces, towering and pressing inward without crevices or ledges for hiding and hunting, the people moving in random herds without direction. The road widened, the noise outside the truck mounting.

Xue Bao heard bells many times louder than the ones on the mountain when the herders drove their flocks, and horns louder still. There was the squalling of a siren, a crescendo of noise as a green car with flashing blue lights above its cloth roof and wipers batting raindrops from the flat windshield swerved through the vehicles on the other side and rushed past, the siren falling as it traveled away. Men in open long yellow coats lacquered with rain stood in the middle of the road. Under the coats were green uniforms with yellow stripes down the legs, white belts, white straps slanted across their chests, and green high-crowned visored caps with red and yellow bands on them. The men raised hands in white gloves and blew shrill whistles. When a gloved hand dropped, horns honked ahead and behind. Sometimes the truck driver honked, too, before lurching on.

They passed buildings with doors opened to the street; and from the doors poured jangled music, not like the distant singing and lute playing Xue Bao heard on the mountain on still nights from the men in black tents and mud-brick houses when they drank barley wine, or even the herders' dogs' gong-like barking that rolled across the slopes of the mountain in the dark. This music came from instruments unimagined by Xue Bao, and the voices were from a kind of human he never heard before. Beneath the music and whistles and horns and sirens was another layer of sound, of the pressure of trucks and cars and motorcycles and all the people walking, the weight of all the buildings pressing on the land, a constant muffled tectonic groan like rock grinding on rock beneath ground or the far off crack and boom of ice breaking on Teal Sea in the spring thaw. It seemed to fill all the space so there was no refuge from noise, while on the mountain there would have been only the sound of wind or the skirling of an eagle or a marmot's barking, all else silence.

Xue Bao never heard so much noise before, and wondered if anyone but he heard it. No one in the crowds seemed to. Among all the people only one or two looked like the herders who lived in the lands below the mountain. There were priests here, instead of shaven-headed nuns who turned the yellow-metal canisters. The priests dressed in crimson robes, their scalps shaved, too, strings of bone beads around their necks or being fingered in their hands, some wearing black-framed eyeglasses. Other men wore white prayer caps and had long wispy beards. Still others had jackets buttoned tight over thick sweaters underneath.

Many of the people carried umbrellas or folded newspapers over their heads in the rain. Beneath umbrellas women with glistening straight black hair hanging far down the backs of their canary jackets wore white masks over their noses and mouths, large dark glasses hiding their eyes. Older children, wearing blue sweaters over white shirts and blue pants or skirts, walked in groups, hurrying through the drizzle, satchels hunched high on their backs. Tiny children, each holding the hand of a grown person with an opened umbrella, were padded in warm clothes of every brilliant color, their heads covered with hoods or knit caps, their cheeks ripe red berries. Almost everywhere were men in green uniforms and long open yellow raincoats.

More trucks and cars crowded the road, and the truck crept forward while the blue-hide man fixed on what was straight ahead. At an intersection stood a round, two-story building with windows and red, yellow, and green lights on it. When the facing light was green, the traffic moved a little way, surging when the light changed to yellow, stopping again with red. The truck sat stopped more than it moved, and the driver lit another cigarette and tapped his hands on the steering wheel.

They lurched a short distance, halted, lurched again. It was late afternoon, and the rain stopped. Xue Bao looked for the sun and saw it through gauze, almost the way it was on the plateau when the wind filled the sky with powdery dust. But the wind had gone down here; and the sky was not the clean copper of highlands three miles above the sea but stained as if by a residue.

The truck halted again. The driver spoke to Xue Bao, asking a question. Xue Bao tried to make a sound like the driver's but only rumbled so low the driver could not hear. The driver asked again, louder, as if Xue Bao were deaf. Xue Bao lifted his right arm, extending the index finger out of the long sleeve, pointing to the sidewalk.

The cars ahead moved. The driver shoved the gearshift. The truck shuddered forward. When it stopped again, Xue Bao opened the door and dropped to the road as the driver yelled. Landing on the balls of his feet without a stumble, Xue Bao stepped up on the curb, turning to watch the truck stop-and-go, the driver twisting, trying to catch sight of Xue Bao again, until the driver and his truck were swept up with all the other trucks and cars and busses and people into the city, the tassels of the knotted red string with masks swinging from the mirror.

Xue Bao had no set direction except onward, and he followed the sidewalk the way the truck had gone. Brown water, rainbows swirling on it, ran down the gutter along the curb. The dark patches on the wet concrete evaporated. He walked without pausing; and the soles of his feet began to burn as they rubbed inside the boots striking the hard sidewalk, and soon his eyes blinked and watered. He breathed through parted lips, his throat scratching and his chest aching.

Xue Bao looked at the faces he passed, none of them seeming to be bothered by the air. Maybe they were accustomed to it, like the driver who filled his lungs with smoke.

Most of the people looked through Xue Bao. A few stopped short when he looked at them, turning their heads away when he held their gazes, as the wolfling had. Xue Bao saw that people did not look into one another's eyes as they hurried past, mute in all the noise.

Shadows stretched out on the sidewalk and road. As the sun lowered, the glass walls of the buildings changed to the color of revolving canisters. Many of the buildings had large glass double doors opening onto the sidewalk. Xue Bao stopped in front of one set. Inside people pushed large wheeled wire baskets or carried plastic ones hanging by handles from their bent arms, walking past shelves filled with things. The people searched the shelves as if they were looking for minor prey upon which to pounce. Pausing, they'd take something down and put it into their baskets, stand a few seconds, then remove it and replace it on the shelf.

Turning away from the glass doors, Xue Bao saw a reflection in them. The reflection stared into his eyes as the people did not. He studied the image in the glass. What he saw in it was not ugly or disfigured, just formed in a way strange in Xue Bao's sight.

From the large fur-lined hat to the wide apart, black, chitinous eyes; white, white teeth; bent nose with a wide scar across the bridge; hollow cheeks roughened and colored by wind, sun, and cold; thin hairs at each corner of his upper lip and on his chin; the coat with sleeves hanging to his thighs; tall black boots, all of it looked cobbled together from random parts. He shifted his gaze to the reflection of the people passing behind, then through the glass to the people inside, and decided he appeared no different, or any worse arranged, than they. To himself, though, he looked as absurd as his bare foot had in the eating place back in the village.

Xue Bao walked on. A man coming toward him rasped a gobbet onto the sidewalk without breaking stride. Xue Bao looked away as he passed, and walked faster until he came to a corner.

Across the street to his left ran a long broad alley.

Small open rooms lined both sides of the alley. Down the center were rows of wooden stalls covered by cloth canopies, people shuttling between stalls and doors. Xue Bao stepped down from the curb.

To one side Xue Bao saw a blue taxi cart moving between the larger cars on the street. He took a step and was out of its way before the driver could honk. A black sedan came in the other direction, and Xue Bao stopped and it passed an inch from him. He saw the driver's contorted face shouting at him from behind the tinted glass. Other horns honked, and Xue Bao stepped onto the opposite curb and into the alley.

The people stopped here to look, talking to one another or with the people inside the rooms or in the stalls. Xue Bao saw that some of the rooms were filled with clothes on hangers or bolts of fabric on tables; others had shoes, music tapes and disks, suitcases, knapsacks, books, large square glass apothecary jars with red-banded snakes floating in clear fluid, or toys of colored plastic. The stalls down the center of the alley were piled with foods Xue Bao knew nothing of.

There were red, orange, and purple fruits, and green and red vegetables. The mountain had none of these, only grass and roots; but many of these might have been unfamiliar to someone who saw fruits and vegetables every day. Big plastic bins were heaped with spices, small white squares of cardboard glued to wooden sticks stuck into different colored, and different smelling, mounds. The prices and names, which Xue Bao could not read, were written in black-ink numerals and swooping hànzi on the cardboard squares.

Behind the stalls people grilled and roasted foods. Trays were filled with polished, brown-skinned chestnuts, the smell hot and sweet. Xue Bao felt their warmth as he passed, like that of a rock in the sun. In other stalls, meat cooked. Xue Bao stopped where a woman in a short black quilted jacket and a white scarf tied around her hair, straight ends of gray showing from beneath, broiled pieces of meat spiked on pale-green bamboo skewers. She sat on a canvas stool, using a yellow paper fan to winnow white ash from red lumps of charcoal in a small black-iron brazier with black-iron rings for handles and three crossed black-iron legs. A green, straight-handlebarred bicycle with a yellow saddle leaned against the back of the stall. Xue Bao smelled the broiling meat, his mouth watering.

Picking up five skewers with one hand, the woman turned them, the meat sizzling and white smoke rising as she placed the skewers back on the grill. She saw Xue Bao watching, and called to him. Xue Bao tilted his head. The woman called again. When he still did not answer, she lifted three skewers and held them toward him, nodding. Xue Bao stepped closer and reached for them, but the woman pulled them back. She said something else, her voice more excited. Laying down the fan, she held up three fingers of that hand. Xue Bao slid his hand into the slit in his coat and brought it out, opening it to show a few circles of metal in his palm.

The woman looked at the metal Xue Bao held and turned away, waving her empty hand at him as she placed the skewers back on the grill. She picked up the fan. Xue Bao stood, his hand extended. Sitting on the stool the woman raised her head. Closing the fan and tucking it into her palm under her little finger and thumb, she waved three fingers at him again, saying something in an angry voice, her other hand clenched. Once more she turned to the brazier, her back to him.

Xue Bao closed his hand and put the metal circles back into his coat pocket. He stood, looking at the meat, then turned to walk off. After a step he heard the woman's voice and looked back to see her, still sitting, the three skewers of cooked meat in her hand, her holding them toward him, not looking at him. Xue Bao walked back and reached to take the skewers from her. His hand touched hers as he did, and she sat up, dropping the fan. Her nostrils flared and she took in a sharp breath as she looked at him. She drew her hand back and clenched the quilted fabric of her jacket with it, rubbing her knuckles with the fingers of her other hand. Xue Bao walked on, carrying the skewers.

The meat cooling, Xue Bao looked for a place to crouch or lie to eat, but there were too many people; so he ate as he walked, tearing the meat from the skewers and letting each fall to the ground like a slender stripped bone as he did. Done, he made sure he wasn't being watched as he licked the grease and juices from his hands, wiping around his mouth with the wetted back of one.

The meat made him thirsty, even more than the way it would on the mountain. One of the stalls had tall plastic bottles of water in cardboard boxes. He gazed at them until the man in the stall came to him and spoke. Xue Bao continued looking at the bottles, and the man got one and held it out, holding his other hand palm up. Xue Bao took the remaining metal from his coat pocket and dropped it into the man's opened hand. The man looked at the metal, shrugged, and handed Xue Bao the bottle. Xue Bao turned back toward the end of the alley.

The bottle had a blue plastic cap, but Xue Bao could not understand how to open it. His fangs could have once punctured it, but he could not bite through with these now blunt teeth. He drew another fang, though, the two-edged metal tongue with white metal figures on the horn handle, and sliced the neck off the bottle, water spraying. He slid the dagger back into its horn sheath. His flesh tongue would not fit inside the bottle to lap, so he lifted it and sealed the opening with his lips, tilted it, and drank. Water bubbled from the bottle until it was empty, and he dropped it on the ground where it made a sound like a drum. People looked at Xue Bao, but none spoke to him.

Through a space between two buildings at the end of the alley, Xue Bao saw the sun going down. It sank behind a thick bank of the gray-brown clouds, the ring of its rim invisible, now only a red glow in the haze. With the sun went the day's warmth, and Xue Bao hunched his shoulders to gather his body's heat inside his coat instead of in amber-gray fur.

There were no more stalls at the end of the alley for Xue Bao to warm himself by. He could go left or right. Left would take him back the way he had come, right would bear him deeper into the city. He turned right, the setting sun on his left and the north ahead, the cold coming out of it.

Blackness overtook the fox-hued sky. On the street and in the buildings lining it, blue electric lights pulsed on, feeble then bright. Xue Bao saw a block of light at the end of the street. When he got closer, there was a bluff-wide screen rising high above the ground, broadcasting changing pictures of smiling men and women, their heads large as covered trucks, white-stone teeth bared; droplets of moisture beading on the surfaces of bottles of colored glass; and giant tilted packages of pure-white cigarettes. From two blocks away he saw that the screen was erected on the roof of a large square building with tall white square columns and wide white steps mounting to a dozen glass-and-yellow-metal doors. White lights strung along the roof and down the sides scaffolded the building in incandescence.

Around the outside, twenty paces from the steps that led to the doors, ran a low fence of iron bars painted white and topped with leaf points. At intervals were tall poles with blue lights making the ground brighter than under the full moon. Cars and taxi carts pulled up to the fence, tires crunching gravel. People got out with suitcases, canvas bags, and boxes and bulging bundles trussed up with blue nylon ropes, and walked through gaps in the fence too narrow for vehicles. They crossed the lighted stones beyond the fence under the ferocious smiling electric faces and flickering packs of cigarettes. Trudging beneath the loads of their rope-tied luggage, they climbed the stairs and disappeared into the doors. Xue Bao came to the fence, walked along it, and passed through one of the gaps.

Past the iron-barred fence, a wide wooden signboard twice Xue Bao's height faced him, a map painted on it. Xue Bao tried to understand the land the map showed but saw only incomprehensible black lines. He walked on toward the building.

Young men sat on the steps of the building. The ones without jackets buttoned the collars of their shirts up to their chins against the cold. Others wore light-green jackets with shoulder flaps. On the sleeves and breasts of the jackets were darker places that once bore insignia, and on the men's heads were light-green fatigue caps. They held the hides of animals draped across their knees.

The hides were soft, white, fleecy, from the kind

of sheep and longhaired goats herders kept. When anyone with his suitcase and bundle started up the stairs, the young men stood and came over to display the hides, stroking their hands through the softness of the hair. None of the people stopped to look, climbing without slowing. The young men followed a few steps, then walked back to where they sat, speaking single words to one another and passing shared brown-paper cigarettes as they waited for the next person.

The young men rose and came toward Xue Bao as he stepped onto the stairs. He stopped. The young men crowded in, flanking him; and his hand fell on the dagger on his belt. They spoke in a rush, showing him their hides, asking him to buy—not knowing he had no more paper or metal, no more bills or coins. They lifted one hide after another from those folded over their arms. Xue Bao did not touch any hides and moved past the young men.

He climbed again; and the young men fell away, except for one without a cap who followed still, hurrying beside him to show him more hides. When they were many steps above the others, the one with Xue Bao stepped in front, blocking him. He lifted the hides on his arm to show him one unlike the others, hidden in the pile. It was small and gray with a line of black hackles. The young man blew on it to reveal the fineness of the fur.

The collar of the young man's light-green shirt was buttoned and his lank unbarbered hair hung over thin eyebrows, his fingers stained where they held cigarettes. When their eyes met, Xue Bao felt a cold sharper than the air and looked away, stepping around him, and the young man hid the pelt back in the pile on his arm and walked down to the other peddlers, wondering why he had bothered to try to sell a herder hides.

At the top of the steps was a wide landing of granite wallowed by the soles of thousands of shoes. Xue Bao crossed it, pushing open a glass-and-yellow-metal door. Past the door, Xue Bao entered a room as large and high as a summit on the mountain, the room oscillating and bourdoning with fluorescence.

People bearing boxes and suitcases crowded the level where he stood, passing in fitful locomotion in and out of large openings in the walls, their raised heads rotating in dismay. Through the openings Xue Bao saw the long black-and-green trains, like the one that crossed the cliff face outside the city. Stands lit with terrible light sold crackers, sweet drinks, newspapers, and candy. People rose to an open upper level on escalating stairways. Inside the vast hall were other screens with pictures, along with boards that showed glowing red hànzi and numerals that flickered over to newer ones every few seconds. Three notes of a chime tolled and a woman's echoing voice spoke above the noise of the great room. White steam and black smoke billowed from a train as it began to chuff and caterpillar backward on its track. People moved in every direction, like green-eyed flies or tiger-headed hornets swarming among the apian drone of electric circuitry.

Xue Bao was passing damp palms over each other. When he realized, he stopped and held his hands at his sides in blue-veined fists. He listened for the empty silence of the mountain, unable to locate it inside him, as he walked back to the glass-and-yellow-metal doors, drew one open, and went out. The young men sitting on the steps did not look at him as he descended the granite steps, Xue Bao telling himself not to run.

Xue Bao saw his breath in the light. Fewer people were on the street as he passed the two-dimensional map of the land and went through a gap in the white fence. He walked without direction, now, turning corners as he came to them, not turning others. Sometimes he was on a busy street with many people and cars and lights, and then he walked down a narrow deserted one with no sidewalks, hearing only his boot soles on the paving stones. From across a narrow street a woman beneath a white light, wearing a short jacket and a tight dress the colors of a pheasant, waved. Xue Bao walked on.

He wandered late into the night until even the widest, brightest-lit streets were almost abandoned by cars and people. He wanted to lie down, but he knew he couldn't in the open. He made another turn, then another, and was on a narrow street with few sounds. Down the center ran a worn cobblestone gutter, gleaming in the scattered light. A high plastered wall, its ancient red paint gray in the dark, ran along one side of the street and in it was an alcove. The opening was six feet deep and sealed by a tall metal door that would not move when Xue Bao pushed it. He leaned against the side of the alcove and rubbed his face against it. It did not have his scent; but the opening was deep enough for him to be in shadow at the back, secreted from passersby in the night. Xue Bao walked in a circle and lay down on his side with his knees drawn in.

Lying on the cement, his eyes heavy, he did not sleep, though he always slept on hard rocky places on the mountain. He sat up, put his back against the metal door, drew up his knees, and wrapped his arms around them to hold in his warmth; but still he did not sleep.

Xue Bao listened to the horns and motors on the wide boulevard a block away, bells and claxons and sirens farther off. Replicated façades of multi-story apartment buildings lined the opposite side of the street. Most windows were dark; but through some a green-gray glow could be seen coating the interiors, and Xue Bao heard faint music and sometimes saw the red flare of a cigarette tip in the darkened rooms.

Tobacco smoke, the cupreous odor of fried meat fat, and a synthesis of unfamiliar fragrances wafted. A kicked bottle clittered over the stones down the street, unbreaking. Listening for dogs, he heard the scratching of tiny claws on stone. A broken-tailed rat, its pelt lustrous in the nightlight, ran in a humped gait down the gutter, stopping to stand on hind legs and scent the air, furless front paws touching limp against its chest, sparkling whiskers twitching.

Dropping back to the ground the rat scurried on down the gutter. A housecat came afterward, padding past the opening and sitting on the curb in front of Xue Bao, its tail wrapped around itself, the tip flicking. Xue Bao watched, knowing the cat did not detect his presence. After a minute, on a whim, Xue Bao made one low growl. The striped cat whirled, spine arched and tail curled, rigid, bristling, hissing as it met Xue Bao's half-lidded eyes with its own unblinking ones, retreating in a panic on the tips of its claws.

Arms around his knees, back against the metal door, Xue Bao sat through the night on the cement. Amid the welter of sounds and scents, he listened for any ones he could identify, scented for ones he knew; but there were none. In the space and quiet of the mountain was emptiness for his senses to fill. Here all was deafening void in which his senses were annulled. Near dawn, Xue Bao slept, in a way.

XUE BAO OPENED his eyes.

The sun had begun to emblazon the apartment buildings, reflecting off the windows and slanting into the alcove, sweeping over Xue Bao, its warmth accentuating the cold of the night. He pushed the palms of his hands against the wall and stood, shrugging his shoulders. Shivering, his neck, back, and knees aching, he hobbled into the daylight, breath steaming.

People moved behind some of the windows across the road, while curtains were drawn across others. Men in tight wool buttoned jackets, carrying rolled net bags, came out of the buildings; women in long dark coats that hung stiff without swaying hurried along the sidewalks, holding the hands of small bright-clothed children, one woman, one child. Bicycles passed, spinning spokes glinting. A man sat rigid on a complaining motor scooter, a white half helmet balanced on his head like an overturned china bowl, a black strap buckled under his chin as he whirred off down the street.

Xue Bao heard the grating of rusted metal behind him. An old man, black hair shot with white, backed through the opened doorway, carrying a large ring of keys. His head was lowered as he closed the metal door and turned a key in the lock. When he looked up Xue Bao was gone, walking along the wall from which faded red paint flaked, never seen by the man in whose alcove he had tried to sleep.

It was half a block before Xue Bao warmed and the stiffness and soreness subsided. He came to a broad street. Cars and motor carts, cycle rickshaws and trucks already moved on it, though fewer than the day before. Ahead of him across the street, old women in black quilted jackets, gray slacks, black cloth slippers, and white head scarves were bent over, sweeping the sidewalk with besoms and tree branches. They swept the cloudy dirt from the sidewalk to the street, a few feet away, working as if it were a matter of some consequence. Xue Bao hesitated, feeling his hunger return.

The women were banded together like sheep, working as if scratching for tubers. They had not seen him; and unlike with the nuns on the plateau, Xue Bao now knew how to kill with what hung on his belt. He looked for a circling route to come up on them into the wind. But the terrain was flat, straight, without variance and features for surprise. He'd have to rush into them, in daylight. How many would he have to kill? Where would he feed, then hide his kill to return to it?

There was something else, though, other than the questions, that kept him from coming off the curb. He saw how he would be walking slow at first as he crossed the street, the women's heads staying down, brooms and branches sweeping, until he was only yards from them when one would look up. Xue Bao would draw the dagger, holding it along his leg until he rushed onto them. The first he came to would still have her head down, and he would batter her onto her back on the sidewalk, his knees pinning her arms, his left hand forcing back her chin and baring her arching throat for the sweep of his right. But the women, he sensed from what he'd seen of humans in the city, would not scatter like the blue sheep. They would fight with branches and brooms while he would have to slash and stab to keep them away. This was prey that would come at too high a cost. He did not know how he knew this, but he did, sharing, somehow, what was in their nature. But even that, he knew, was not why he did not move across the street, but only stood, watching. There was something more, something not yet accessible to him.

A sweeping woman stood, stretching her back.

She saw Xue Bao on the other sidewalk. He was a herder, a bumpkin clothed in mountain dress, staring as if he had never seen a sidewalk or a paved road or automobile before, his right hand on something on the wide belt around his waist. She was going to point him out to the women beside her—look, another one from the country, giving up on country ways; but he had already started walking again, taking his hand from his hip, moving past them on his side of the street. The woman watched until Xue Bao was far down the block.

The rain of the day before had not washed the sky; but in the morning's cold the air was not yet dark-tinged, only gray-hazed. Xue Bao had eaten just the few bites at the woman's stall since his meal in the village and had nothing now to pay for food, or words to ask for it. Along the street were large glass windows; and through them Xue Bao saw clothing, paper, brushes and ink, radios, pots and pans, and meat. Birds picked of their feathers, their bumpy skins sheening in dry pellicles, hung head down on hooks. Cuts of other, skinned animals hung beside them. Xue Bao almost did not recognize his own strange image in the glass as he stared. He pushed and pulled the doors beside the windows, but they would not open.

Xue Bao walked through the morning, seeing wider gaps between the cars and trucks on the street. There were fewer people around in the city, seeming in less of a hurry than the day before. As the morning ebbed, he saw through gilt-lettered windows people eating in shops along the sidewalks. They sat at round tables, bowls of thick ivory noodles in front of them. Large metal bowls rested in holes in the centers of the tables, rings of blue gas flame heating them from below. The liquid in the bowls bubbled while the people with wooden sticks like the village woman used picked from the bowls meat and fish, some of it taloned feet and combed heads, boiled pink, the people waving the sticks in the air as they talked between mouthfuls of food.

Near noon Xue Bao heard poppings, like the noises of the long metal-and-wood stick-guns. Instead of being frightened, Xue Bao was drawn to the noises and saw a man and a woman climb from a low car in front of a shop with a black-bead curtain over the entrance. The man wore a buttoned deep-blue jacket and deep-blue trousers, with a white shirt and red tie and polished black shoes and a white flower in his lapel, while the woman wore a clinging, high-collared, sleeveless and shimmering red cheongsam that fell to the tops of her shiny high-heeled shoes and was slit on the sides to above the knees of her stockinged legs. Her hair shone like black lumps of coal and was pinned up with a red blossom. Both the man and woman had shy smiles, the woman's lips red as the dress and blossom, her face whitened with powder, eyelashes long and as black as her hair. She held the long stems of lilies with both hands; and a group of people, many of the men cradling white-labeled green-glass bottles in the crooks of their arms, stood on either side of the entrance, facing the man and woman, smiling and applauding. On the sidewalk packs of lighted firecrackers jumped, exploding with white flashes, sounding like gunshots. As the man and woman passed through the bead curtain held open for them, the poppings died, flecks of burst red and gray paper blowing down the concrete sidewalk.

Xue Bao had not seen happiness before. On the mountain there was hunger, hunting, eating, mating, sleep, birth, and death, but no possibility, or need, of happiness. Or sadness. The mountain had only being, the being he had abandoned. He watched everyone enter through the bead curtain, then he walked on.

In a quieter district of the city, Xue Bao stood on a corner, seeing no trucks or cars for blocks. A man pedaling a bicycle crossed in front of him. The man was thin, arms and legs like lengths of pipe, wearing loose white clothes, rubber boots outside his trousers, a white prayer cap on his head. The bike had a big square wire basket on the handlebars and extending over the front wheel. The basket carried the dressed and skinned carcasses of three young sheep, lidless glazed eyes gazing from naked black-veined heads. The man pedaled on. Xue Bao turned the corner and followed.

Xue Bao walked fast, not running, but keeping the cyclist in sight. The sun turned the sky brighter and grimier. The rider, a block ahead of Xue Bao, braked at the curb and dismounted. The man wheeled the bicycle onto the sidewalk, pushing down a stand with his rubber-booted foot. Another man, heavy, head square with deep wrinkles around his eyes, with a grizzled beard and shaven upper lip, came out of the shop door. He wore a long white blood-smeared coat and a prayer cap. He spoke to the thin man, then lifted one of the skinned sheep and hoisted it over his shoulder, carrying it into the shop.

As the man came out of the shop again, Xue Bao walked up. The carcasses remaining in the basket were pink and white, the clouded corneas of sunken eyes refracting aqua in the daylight, blackened lipless teeth gritted in fierce grins. Through the long slits of their open bellies Xue Bao saw yellow ribs, covered by a clean taut dry film. The thin man had his back to Xue Bao and did not notice him, but the heavy man did. The thin man turned, directed by the glance of the heavy man. After a silence the heavy man spoke to Xue Bao in a loud voice. When Xue Bao made no sound, the heavy man said something from the side of his mouth. The thin man laughed, and they paid no more attention to Xue Bao.

The heavy man picked up the second sheep and carried it into the shop. Through the glass window, Xue Bao saw him reach to hang it by its hind leg on a large steel hook set higher than his head, the carcass swinging when he released it. There were dozens of whole carcasses hanging in the shop and portions of larger animals and more plucked birds on tables, more animals than Xue Bao could kill in months. He tried to understand what only two men needed with so many.

Xue Bao remembered the other shops with animals. How many places like those were in this city, how many with animals, skinned and pink and white, hanging from steel hooks? Looking at his boots, he thought of all the animals in shoes, belts, and fleece on the bodies of all the people, the hides on the arms of the young men on the stone steps, in numbers that seemed impossible. He wondered where the people hunted all these animals. After his journey in the truck, Xue Bao could not imagine that there was any such place near the city to kill with such wantonness. None in an entire land. Here they had gone beyond whatever he knew on the mountain, Xue Bao never having seen a herder butcher one animal. The scale of such slaying exceeded his envisioning, and he wanted to believe these people must be different from him, that his predator's heart was not like the slaughterers' of this city. Xue Bao remembered, then, what he had done on the mountain, the sheep lost and wasted.

The heavy man came out of the shop. Xue Bao looked at him, searching for the difference. But when he could see none, all he felt was fury, sudden and enveloping, searing away his hunger but not his impulse to strike. These men had killed enough for themselves.

When the heavy man came near the bicycle, Xue Bao pounced, thrusting his arms from long sleeves and grabbing the carcass of the small sheep from the wire basket, then leaping back. Both men stood startled before they began to shout. They started for him, and Xue Bao showed his teeth and made a loud hiss. They halted; and Xue Bao ran, the bouncing carcass cold and stiff on his shoulder.

After a moment the two men gave chase, the heavy man loping some distance before falling back, leaving the pipe-legged thin man to pursue Xue Bao. The thin man shouted; but there were no other people on the street. After a block, though, Xue Bao saw ahead of him white belts and straps and green uniforms. A passageway ran to Xue Bao's left and he pitched down it. Coming out onto a sidewalk, he spun left and after a few hundred feet dashed across the street and ran into a narrow alley. Coming out he found more turns and alleys and passages, and behind him shrill whistles.

Xue Bao leapt into an alley curving to the right. Rounding the bend, he confronted a cul-de-sac ending in a rough wall of concrete blocks, nine feet tall. With the rigid carcass on his shoulder he ran at the wall. He jammed his left boot toe against it and pushed up, reaching for the top with his free right hand. Grabbing the wall, he felt pressure and burning, then sharp pain. He reached for the wall with his left hand, holding onto the edge with the tips of his fingers, holding the palm of his hand away from the top. He strained to pull himself up. The sheep slid from his shoulder, and he tried to snatch it, the hind leg slipping through his wet right hand and the carcass thudding to the alley below. Xue Bao hung on the wall, looking at the lost food. Whistles and running feet drew closer. He lifted his head and saw a fine bead of his own blood rolling down the wall and another twining around his right wrist. He pulled harder.

Not even the sharpest, feathered edge of broken rock on the mountain had ever cut his paw, and Xue Bao could not understand what made him bleed. When his head came to the top of the wall, he saw the jagged foliage of clear and tinted broken glass embedded along it, his blood sparkling on the razor edge of one shard. Swinging his left foot onto the wall, he slid the boot toe between two of the shards. He spread the fingers of his left hand between several pieces of glass without touching them and pulled up, drawing his right foot behind. Standing, he saw two green-uniformed men and the thin man in his white prayer cap coming around the curve of the alley, raising their heads as they saw him on the wall.

They rushed toward him, shouting and blowing whistles. Xue Bao danced along the top of the wall, weaving through the blades of glass, bristling like the dermal plates on the spine of some fossil being, Xue

Bao licking the blood from his lacerated hand as he went. The wall ran eighty feet along the windowless backs of buildings. Halfway, he glanced behind. He could hear the voices of the three men where they stood around the sheep carcass, imagining them looking from it to the wall, arguing, no one willing to scale the wall as Xue Bao had and pursue him through the glass. (Or perhaps they argued about dividing the sheep, prepared to say the outland stranger had absconded with it.)

Xue Bao wove his feet along the wall, hunting for a place to jump from it. Spaces only wide as gutters ran between the wall and buildings. The wall ran into another, higher wall topped with more broken glass. Where the walls met was a narrow passage to the left along the side of a building, with paper and windblown debris in it and just wide enough for him to slip down. The passage led to the street, cars passing. Xue Bao stepped off the wall as if stepping off the tread of a stair, dropping to the ground. Landing with a slight bend of his legs, he ran through the litter, scenting the urine and feces of humans and animals, and slowed to a walk at the end of the passage.

To his right, far down the street as Xue Bao came out onto the sidewalk, a man in a green uniform and cap, his hands braced against the door of a dull-green car set high off the road on large tires, talked through the lowered side window under the car's fabric roof, the car so high the man did not have to bend to speak, even while standing on the sidewalk. On the mountain, humans meant nothing. Now Xue Bao had to flee from them. While the man went on talking, Xue Bao turned left, staying close to the building. No green uniforms or high-sitting cars were ahead.

He did not turn at the first corner but made himself walk to the second and turn right, crossing the street, going straight ahead, walking faster when he thought he was out of sight. At the next corner he turned left, then right at the corner after that. He jogged in the single direction in his mind, away, winding through the city for half an hour, the blood starting to stanch.

On a back street Xue Bao saw a high dull-green car passing at the end of it. He slid into a doorway before the uniformed men looked his way. He waited several seconds, leaned out, and watched for several more, then turned and walked back the way he came.

Xue Bao had to find concealment and refuge till darkness fell. He turned the next corner to the left. Halfway down the street was a five-story block building, surrounded by a brick wall and with a closed gate of tall, gray-painted iron bars. Above the gate rose a sign, made of wrought black metal bars, displaying the name of the building in hànzi. Xue Bao wondered if the building was for the green-uniformed men. The gate rolled open on a whining steel track; and a blue car with no roof lights or large tires drove out, the gate rolling closed behind as the car accelerated away. Xue Bao walked past. There was a parking area for many cars, but just two were there. He looked at the windows in the building above the brick wall, and they were closed and the lights were off behind them.

The wall turned away from the street and ran along the side of the building. Between the wall and the next building was a space Xue Bao could slide down sideways. Along the building above the top of the wall was a pivoted window of pebbled glass, the bottom tilted out. No light was lit in the room behind. Xue Bao looked out to the street, looked back, crouched, and jumped to reach the top of the wall, gripping no more than the edge with his fingertips. He pulled himself up to where he saw embedded shards of jagged glass again, and got his feet onto the wall without cutting himself.

The bottom of the window was at the height of his head, and the wall stood six feet from the side of the building. Xue Bao took a breath. He leaped.

Catching the sill, Xue Bao pulled up, and jackknifed in, squeezing through with his bulky clothes. He rolled to his feet, staying crouched, fingers touching the floor. His eyes adjusted to the dark, and he saw that the floor was made of small squares of black and white tiles, some missing, others cracked, with gray grout between. The room was small. In one corner of the floor was a mop basin and a large gray-metal utility sink with a faucet and handles hung on the wall beside it. Across the room was a porcelain rectangle in the floor with an opening in the center and ribbing on the flats of the rectangle on either side of the hole, a vertical chromed-metal pipe running down the wall behind it and a plastic wastebasket with, his nose told him, fouled paper in it just beside. A rag mop, wrung into a hank and smelling of ammonia, rested in an empty bucket. Xue Bao rose. A filament of light framed a door.

Opening the door the width of one sable eye, Xue Bao saw he was at the end of a long linoleum-floored corridor, numbered closed rooms lining either side. At his end of the corridor was a stairwell, the light-gray wall painted halfway up in shiny lime enamel, stairs ascending and doubling back to climb to the next floor. Three dusty ceiling bulbs lighted the corridor.

Xue Bao watched and listened the way he might have on the mountain, bellied out on a rock above a slope, his only movement his eyes and the shallow expansion of his chest as he breathed through his opened mouth, pink tongue tip extended. The rooms were unlit. There were no noises except the muffled workings of the building. Closing the door without a sound, Xue Bao stood till his dark vision returned. He was as thirsty as he had ever been and needed to drink.

Water dripped from the goose-necked faucet above the utility sink. Xue Bao looked at it. After several moments he reached out with his uncut hand and touched one of the handles. He pulled it toward him and there was a rattling, then a sputtering, and water spat from the faucet, flowing. As Xue Bao bent forward, he saw that the water had begun to steam. He stood up, pushing the handle back. He looked at the other handle and pulled it.

Xue Bao let the water run from the faucet, waiting for steam. When there was none, he bent and turned his head, putting his mouth near the surge and lapping. For more than a minute he lapped until he filled his stomach with cold iron-tasting water. Standing, he pushed the handle, halting the water. He kept his hand there. He pulled the handle again and cocked his head, watching the water splash into the sink and swirl down the drain hole. Xue Bao pushed the handle back. Then pulled it once more. Shutting off the water, he went to the door. Cracking it a sliver, he scanned the corridor, then opened the door and slipped from the room.

Along the corridor some of the doors had small windows with wire mesh sandwiched in the panes. Through the windows Xue Bao saw steel tables and vitrines framed in white enameled metal, shining instruments, and specimen jars, large and small, with glass stoppers. Suspended in the vessels were whole frogs, serpents, fish, and individual organs, animal and human.

Midway down the corridor, Xue Bao looked at his right hand. Pulling himself through the window had reopened the wound. On the linoleum floor, beetle-back asterisks of red gleamed along his trail. He bent his arm, raising his hand, palm inward. The blood pearled down his forearm, demarcating a coagulating line that vanished into the sleeve of his coat. Through the window of one of the doors he saw white cloths folded on a brushed-steel table. The brass knob turned in his left hand and the door opened. Still elevating his right hand, he listened for the sound of anyone in the room before opening the door all the way and entering.

Xue Bao crossed to the table and took a cloth, snapping it open. Biting a corner he tore down a long strip and wrapped his bleeding hand, knotting the loose ends snug. For a moment he looked at the knot. He did not know how he knew to tie it. He lowered his hand.

Listening first at the door, he went back into the corridor, latching the door behind. A door opened and closed on the floor below. Footsteps echoed in the stairwell, ascending.

Xue Bao retreated, eyes on the stairwell and reaching behind to try the knobs along the corridor. Some were locked. Others were open, but the rooms beyond the doors were bare of hiding places. He backed the length of the corridor, to a windowless door at the end. The scuffing of shoes on the steps amplified, and the top of a man's black-haired head appeared in the stairwell against the gloss of the lime paint.

Reaching behind, Xue Bao found the knob. It turned. Without letting the knob make a click, he opened the door and slid into the room. Once more he left the door open, now pupil wide, to see a man with black-framed glasses climb out of the stairwell. The man was dressed in a white shirt and blue denims and a down-filled red jacket zipped closed. In one hand was a worn leather satchel and in the other a dozen sheets of blue onionskin held together by a metal clip. He had folded back the top sheets and read as he walked in a deliberate pace.

At the third door from the stairwell the man stopped and put down the satchel. He took keys from his pocket, making a light contemplative jangling as he went on reading. A blue sheet crackled as he turned it. Without looking, he felt for a key on the ring, scratched it over the doorknob, and found the keyhole. Turning the key, he pushed open the door and walked in. He was swinging the door closed behind him when he halted. Glancing over his shoulder, he turned around.

Walking back into the corridor, the man bent to pick up the satchel. His hand was almost on the soft, darkened leather handle, the clipped papers in the other, when he lifted his head. Without picking up the satchel he stood, staring at the spattered string of Xue Bao's blood along the floor.

Retracing the trail down the corridor, the man opened the door of the room with the utility sink. Reaching in he threw a switch that turned on a light.

He hesitated then looked in. He searched the room with his eyes. The pebble-glassed window was open, and drops of blood and water were on the floor; but the room was empty. The man switched off the light and closed the door. Turning, he followed the droplets to the room where Xue Bao had gotten the cloth. Opening the door, he looked in, then closed the door. Now he turned and looked to the other end of the corridor. He began walking toward Xue Bao's door.

Xue Bao sank back into the room, closing the door without a sound. Through the closed door he heard the man opening the unlocked doors along the corridor and using his keys to open the locked ones, his steps nearing. Xue Bao breathed through his teeth, listening to the man's steps.

The room had no windows. No light came in around the door, so that for a long time even Xue Bao's eyes would not let him see anything but lighter black against blacker black. Then the lighter black began to assume forms, mute and immobile.

Xue Bao turned from the door and flattened against the wall, sliding along it, trying to identify the shapes as he drew away from them. There was a familiarity to them, even in the blackness, but in the way of fabrications. As he slid along the wall, his shoulder pushed against a switch, moving it up.

Glass tubes in the ceiling hummed and flared with fluorescence, flickered off, then blinked on until they came all the way on and lit the room.

It appeared larger than Xue Bao had sensed in the blackness. And it was even more crowded with figures, the number seeming an endless multiple. It took time for him to realize that mirrors from floor to ceiling lined two opposite walls, creating a reflected infinity.

It was not a reflection facing Xue Bao, though, but a wild ass, eyes bulged with terror and mouth gaped wide, sallow donkey's ivories exposed. Stunned, Xue Bao waited for the ass to bray, to kick in fright; but it did not move. The ass's mouth stayed open, its eyes round, the long head thrown back, cracked translucent front hooves and bald-patched cannons thrust forward, skeletal knees and hocks braced. It stood as if hammered to its wooden stand where it had been left to die and rigor.

Beside the wild ass listed a great wild argali sheep, horns curling in five-foot geometric spirals, the tawed hide of its muzzle fissured, exposing yellow straw inside. Behind the ass on rigid legs stood a wild yak bull, bloated and set, as if drowned in a spring torrent of turbid water and filled with mud that hardened. A white-lipped deer, a hind without the stag's tall six-tined antlers, had its tattered ears straight up, like an ass's. A little goat-like serow stood beside the deer, smaller than a deer's fawn. The only smaller animal was a tan-and-white gazelle, standing in front of the serow. And in front of the gazelle stood a blue-sheep ram. All were distorted, deformed, ragged, dingy, desiccated; all motionless

and voiceless; monstrosity and dumbness repeated in the eternity of mirrors.

How could they have all lived here, captive in this windowless, airless room? No, they had lived someplace else, and there the killing had been done, and their hides taken and brought here and rubbed with alum and stuffed with straw and sewn with thick needles and coarse thread into travesties. So they now went on, eating and drinking nothing, touching nothing, feeling nothing, glass eyes never closing or blinking, no sounds made or breaths taken, lungs snatched from within; no flush of warmth, hearts discarded.

Better, Xue Bao thought, for wolves to have pulled them down while their pulses still tripped and to have torn them open, to lick the blood of them from their paws on the high plateau under the moon. Better in the daylight to have the eagles and griffons and choughs sail down and slip under the rent hides and pluck the meat, sand foxes slinking in among them to pilfer, until only bones lay, disjoined and crumbling white, to blow away after the weathering of repeated summers and winters.

A floor-to-ceiling cabinet with glass casement doors stood across the room from Xue Bao. Behind the glass were five shelves. Like the pile on the brushed-steel table in the other room, thick folded cloths were stacked on the shelves, three or four on each. Unlike those other cloths, though, these were not white—not all white. In amber-gray fur large black rosettes floated.

Xue Bao knew he had been looking at them since the lights came on but not seeing them. Their presence filled the room as the fur of his mother had once filled his lair, but without warmth. Staring at them through the glass, he thought of the young man on the steps with the pile of hides draped on his arm, and all the dead animals hanging behind windows. Then, as he studied the too-well-known, unmistakable pattern of spots on one of the pelts, drops dripped in incontinent horror down his inner leg.

The knob turned. Xue Bao's head snapped away from the glassed-in shelves as the door opened, and he threw himself backward, shattering a mirrored panel into quicksilvered shards. The black-framed glasses appeared in the doorway. The man dropped his keys, his other hand crushing the sheaf of onionskin pages.

The last pieces of the mirror disintegrated around Xue Bao and showered the floor, breaking again as the two looked into each other's eyes. Then the man's eyes went to Xue Bao's clawed hands, the right, wrapped in the strip of knotted white cloth seeping blood, moving toward his belt; and as the man's eyes widened, Xue Bao's fear left. His lips drew back from his teeth. Then it filled him, a word.

Xue Bao shouted it at the man as he pounced: "Beast!"

The man uttered a thin cry. Like a panicked blue

sheep he turned and fled, the sheets of onionskin fluttering in his hand like blue flags on poles and ropes. Xue Bao's hands opened as he bounded after the man, but the man ran fast. His cry mounted to a shriek as he ran, and Xue Bao understood he was pleading for help. The man twisted his head back at Xue Bao, his mouth and eyes agape, as wide as the wild ass's; and his foot caught on the satchel he had left on the floor. His arms wheeled as he flew and crashed to the floor, his forehead striking the linoleum. The clipped onionskins fluttered like a blue-feathered bird stooped on by a falcon and tumbling to earth. The man slid on the floor, then lay without moving.

Xue Bao landed, planting his feet on either side of the man's red-jacketed back. Clasping the man's black hair in both hands, he pulled his head back. Blood pooled on the floor from the wound on the man's forehead, drops dripping into the pool. Xue Bao took his right hand from the man's hair and brought it to his dagger.

After capturing, killing for Xue Bao had always been immediate and sure. But something else was within him now, rather than the calm and pure nothingness he always knew at the finish of a chase; something from the place where the word came, something that made him feel outrage and hatred (neither ever felt before, not for the other animals on the mountain—not even wolves—or for any other human he had seen, and might have killed and eaten). But it was not the outrage and hatred themselves. It was the knowledge of them, incarnated in him. Outrage and hatred were the scent marks, the spoor; but it was the trail they led him down, and the place they seemed to be leading him—to such disgust for these creatures that it was the killing itself he desired, not what the killing brought. He wanted to kill, instead of needing to. It was a sense that should have been alien to him deep into his veins and nerves. But it was here, making his skin horripilate and him hesitate, without his understanding why.

Hands, these hands, and teeth, these teeth, were inadequate. But Xue Bao had a single claw, a single sufficient fang, on his belt. But in that instant when he could have drawn it he did not, uncertain, fearful of, and repulsed by, the crafted steel blade. Then he heard yelling from the floor below, the sound of running on the stairs.

Letting go of the man's hair, Xue Bao straightened; and as he did, the man's head began to rock from side to side. His hands flexed, and he moaned. At the other end of the corridor was another stairwell. Xue Bao leaped toward it as the other men came up the far one.

Vaulting the railing, Xue Bao dropped to the flight of stairs below and ran down it. At the bottom was an entrance area with glass doors that opened onto steps leading to the place where the cars were parked. Springing at the doors, he fell back from them. They were locked, and he had nothing with which to break the thick glass. Anxious, tentative voices were in the stairwell, descending.

Xue Bao turned. Numbered doors lined both sides of another corridor, all the knobs with locks in them. He had no time to check for open ones.

Looking under the stairs, Xue Bao saw in the shadows at the back, below the bottom of the soffit slanting down along the concrete wall, an unfinished gap two feet high and four feet wide, eight feet above the floor. Xue Bao didn't wait but ran and jumped, pulling himself in his heavy clothing into the gap.

Inside, the space was four feet deep. Clumps of dust, the dried husks of insects, and loose bits of concrete and plaster littered it. Pressed in, Xue Bao turned himself around to face out and drew as far back into the darkness as he could.

The voices and footsteps reached his floor. Two men held a murmured argument about where the attacker had gone. One said that they should search for him; the other said, no, they should wait for the police. They went silent. The dust filled Xue Bao's nose, but he did not move. He was not surprised to have understood the men's words.

One of the men whispered that perhaps they ought to go back and see how the injured man was; but the other, who had said they should wait for the police, said the man would be all right and that another person was with him. He told the man with him that they should stay together. In case. They did not speak anymore and seemed to remain in the same spot in the middle of the entrance area, shifting from foot to foot, close to each other, breathing in rhythm.

Ten minutes later, breathing almost not at all, Xue Bao heard a sharp tap on glass and the excited voices of the two men as they hurried toward the doors. Keys made a loud jangling as a lock turned. A glass door whooshed open. The two men talked over each other until the voice of a green-uniformed man (because even though he could not see him, that is who Xue Bao knew it must be) rose above, ordering them to speak one at a time.

What had happened, the green-uniformed man asked. Their colleague had been attacked? Who attacked him? Describe him. A mad herdsman from the country? Was he still in the building?

The men did not know. The green-uniformed man asked if they had called an ambulance, and the two men said nothing. Where was he, the green-uniformed man asked, the injured man? He was with another colleague upstairs, they said. The green-uniformed man sighed. We shall see if the man needs assistance, then search the building. You said he was upstairs?

The two men said yes, together, and Xue Bao heard steps on the stairs. They reached the upper floor. The echoing voice of the green-uniformed man asked the wounded man how he was, and Xue

Bao could hear a faint groan of distress.

As Xue Bao was about to pull himself from the space and drop to the ground, a light beam painted the underside of the stairs. Xue Bao drew back. The top of a high-crowned cap, of a second green-uniformed man who had been silent, followed the light under the stairs. In a moment the man would find something to stand on, or jump up, his light filling Xue Bao's hiding place. Time was gone.

Knocking the green-uniformed man to the ground as he hurled himself on him, Xue Bao heard the air rush out of him. As the green-uniformed man lay gasping on the floor, Xue Bao was up and shoving through the unlocked glass doors, jumping from the front steps, running across the wide parking area (a dull-green car with a fabric roof, parked across the closed gate) to the fence of tall iron bars painted gray.

Xue Bao heard shouts and whistles behind him as he leapt to the hood of the green car and reached the top of the fence, hoisting himself over. The ends of the bars were pointed; and as he dropped on the other side, a point pierced the sleeve of the coat, missing his arm. Xue Bao hung by one arm on the outside of the fence as it rolled, squealing, open.

Two green-uniformed men, one bent forward holding in his hand his high-crowned visored cap with the red-and-yellow band (his other hand against his stomach), ran toward him, the two men without green uniforms standing back on the steps of the building. Xue Bao yanked at the coat's sleeve and with a loud rip tore himself free, dropping to the ground.

Long sleeves flapping, Xue Bao ran, knowing without looking back or having to hear their whistles that the green-uniformed men followed. Xue Bao threw himself down the first passageway between buildings, running with half-bounding strides. Coming out on a side street, he went left without thinking, finding a passageway and dashing down it, coming out again on another street and making a sharp turn to the right.

Xue Bao went up an alley. A tall wooden sawhorse barricade, painted white with a red lantern hanging unlit from it, blocked the way. Xue Bao ducked beneath the barricade, putting a hand down to keep from sprawling. Ahead, the old cobblestones of the alley were pried up from side to side and for twenty feet along it. The excavation went down fifteen feet, and in it Xue Bao saw bricks of ancient walls, then layers of stones, metal and clay pipes crisscrossed, the soil gray and crumbling, at the bottom an oily pool of water reflecting a rippling cottony disk of the sun and the blur of his own reaching arms and outstretched legs as he hurdled the gap.

Out on another street, Xue Bao turned down another winding passageway between buildings and found it ending in a tall chain-link fence. Behind and along the fence was a stand of thick bamboo growing. Xue Bao looked back. No one followed, and he had outrun the sound of whistles. He waited a minute, watching and listening as his breathing eased, then scaled the fence.

The fence was taller than the gate of iron bars. On its top, though, was nothing to stab or cut him. He went over it and dropped to the ground inside the bamboo. He crouched and moved through the towering green stalks away from where he had scaled the fence, not rustling the leaves. Coming to a little hollow, he thought he had gone far enough. He got down on all fours, his breathing and his heart slowing until they were normal.

Sweat lay beneath his fur-lined cap and curled down the furless skin along his spine, something never felt before. Now the sweat chilled him and he shivered. When he stopped shivering, he crawled to the edge of the bamboo.

A meadow of grass, browning and with patches of bare dirt, spread in front of him in the afternoon, the air above looking washed. Scattered willows and elms grew in it, and brick paths serpentined through. A small lake was in the middle, an island of tall porous spirit rocks, like castle turrets bored by stone-eating white ants, rising from it. Ducks were on the island and in the lake and on the shore. Undisturbed, they waddled, chattered in the lake as they paddled and fed, stood on the shore on one webbed orange foot with the other tucked up, or lay on plump downy bellies, sleeping in the late-afternoon light, their heads turned back and resting on folded wings, yellow bills slipped beneath white flight feathers.

In the arid country of the mountain Xue Bao had seen ducks, wild ones, sometimes from the highest ridges, the birds in skeins, heading south through the ice-white winter sky or north in the dust-shrouded sky of spring. Unlike those ducks that were always out of reach, these looked too fat to fly more than mere yards; and Xue Bao remembered his hunger.

More than ducks and trees, though, it was people who filled the meadow. In one grassy place rows of men and women made slow movements in unison, as if rolling a huge invisible ball or stroking the side of a tall unseen horse. Along the paths, others in ones and twos pushed carriages, the heads of the babies and small children in them covered in knit caps; or they carried babies in cradles strapped to their backs or chests. Many walked with older children, never more than one with each pair of adults, the children sometimes holding a long string, a floating balloon towed at its end, the children in warm clothes in the colors of balloons. Young men and women walked together holding hands, heads down, not daring to look at each other except in bashful glances; older men and women without children walked side by side, arms held behind backs; old people walked alone or sat on benches, some leaning on sticks, like tottery derricks.

A man stood alone, looking up. A wooden wheel with a crank hung flat from straps on his shoulders, the wheel holding hundreds of feet of string, the string played out so far into the clean-looking sky it sagged like telephone wire. High at the end of the string was a round, winged kite with a bird's beaked head and fanned tail, satin streamers fluttering from the tips of the wings and the end of the tail, the kite slipping in the wind, as small as a gliding faraway bird of prey. Passersby looked up at the man's kite, their lips parted. No one hurried here, no one raised his voice. Xue Bao heard laughter carrying kindness.

Xue Bao saw an old woman in a black coat, her face with deep wrinkles, walking on two sticks. At each of her elbows was a long-black-haired young woman, supporting her. They walked without speaking, the two young women mirroring each slow step of the old woman's, looking ahead to where the old woman would place her foot, making sure the way was clear. It was strange to Xue Bao to see such age, or the young helping the old. On the mountain life ended before true old age. And it ended alone.

While Xue Bao watched these mysterious beings, the string of a balloon slipped from the hand of a small child. The child's parents threw balls of bread to the ducks splashing in the lake and did not see the child trot in somber silence after the balloon drifting toward the bamboo. The balloon escaped over the top of the bamboo as the child, awkward in his padded clothes, waddled to the edge of the stand, his eyes raised to the blue sky. Xue Bao gathered himself up in the shadows of the hollow.

The small child lowered his eyes from the sailing balloon. Xue Bao felt the beat of his heart climb. The child peered into the dark bamboo. He saw two sparks of eye-shine reflected from mirrored retina. Xue Bao gauged the distance, shifting his weight onto his bent legs, his bound hand poised on the dagger's handle. Seconds passed, and the child, trembling now, remained fixed; but Xue Bao did not pounce. His eyes were seeing not the child but an inner vision of contradiction and chaos. Was this what humans carried within them? Did they have a word for it? For Xue Bao it was only a kind of madness they must fight to keep hidden, for their species to survive.

The spark of this madness dimmed in Xue Bao's eyes; and the child, looking into them, blinked. Without a sound the child spun and ran back to his parents. He squirmed his way between their close-beside hips and took the hand of each, too young to know, yet, what reflection he had seen, still trembling within his warm clothing, his balloon adrift in the sky and from his mind.

Xue Bao sat back on his haunches, feeling a sickening lightness. He sank into the hollow and lay on his belly, gathering leaf fall with his elbows and knees to fashion a nest. He turned twice and curled his body, his chin on his crossed wrists, wanting his eyes to stay open as they drifted closed.

HUNGER AWOKE XUE BAO. Dark had fallen. The nest was scattered under him, as if he'd thrashed in his sleep. His palms were damp, and the cut beneath the dirty knotted cloth burned. He lay motionless, clenching his hands, trying to identify where and who he was. He remembered he had dreamed.

He had tried not to sleep with the threat of people just beyond the bamboo. He could not remember when he stopped trying. On the mountain the slightest sound or scent awakened him in an instant, guarding his life. Here he had slept through all the noise and smells, as if sleep were preparing a place for death beside it.

The dream had contained definite things, disconnected: water, eyeglasses glinting, firecrackers bursting on a sidewalk, a man in a tall-visored cap, the wheel of a bicycle, a hornless blue sheep, a mountain peak, arms that would not move and a dagger that could not be wielded. None of it held any meaning for Xue Bao; but it all lingered in memory, the sole remembered dream in his life.

He sat up, resting his elbows on his knees and his forehead on the heels of his palms. His bent fingers pressed into his soft hat. In his head now were words, speaking thoughts. Xue Bao had their words; and with their blood he would become their blood, unless he fled this fugitive place, to return to the mountain, to surrender, to be a beast of a different kind.

After a few moments Xue Bao got to his feet and went to the edge of the bamboo. A lattice of spear-shaped leaves hung in front of his eyes as he looked into the meadow. He watched until he was sure the meadow was empty, then parted the leaves and stepped out.

Xue Bao walked to the lake under the gibbous moon. As he drew near, the ducks sleeping on the shore stirred, standing, shaking short looped tails. They had shown no notice of the people around them during the day; but as Xue Bao approached they flew from the lake's edge, quacking in alarm as they labored into the air, unfamiliar with flight. Others pushed into the water, silver wakes purling on white breasts, paddling to escape.

At the lake's edge Xue Bao knelt, lowering his

head to the water, lapping until his belly was full and the hunger quenched, for the time. Standing on the shore, he looked at the black pylons of the spirit rocks on the lake's island. Across the rising moon a bat fluttered like a fallen leaf wind-lifted, more bats appearing.

Xue Bao walked. Circling the shore, he found a ditch at the far end, carrying the water to the lake. He walked up the ditch. From the meadow the city outside seemed stilled, free of sirens or horns. Xue Bao could see its glow, but not the direct glare of its lights. He stopped to watch and listen, then went on till he came to a chain-link fence without bamboo in front of it, the ditch running under it.

Xue Bao crawled under the fence by the ditch. On the other side was an almost dry riverbed with a narrow channel of water meandering down it, shoals of trash piled in it. Xue Bao walked up the watercourse through the night until he came to a smaller tributary of fresh water flowing in. He left the old river for the new ascending one. As he went higher, the river filled from bank to bank; and Xue Bao climbed out, walking on the tops of the large tumbled rocks that formed the bank, hopping from one to the other. As he leapt he remembered the way a swinging tail kept his balance, without his having to think.

After a time Xue Bao recognized this as the river he had seen from the blue-hide man's machine as they traveled toward the tall buildings, the river that ran over rocks and foamed white, ice stepped on the edges. He came to the canyon where the men broke tablets of granite, empty now in the dark. Xue Bao saw the cut running high along the canyon wall. He knelt once more, lapping water from a small eddy to fill the emptiness in his belly, then left the river and scaled the talus, pushing off from one loose rock spilling from beneath a boot to catch a foothold on the one above, his rapid climb sending a fall of rocks down the steep slope. Reaching the cut, he walked along the track laid on it, stepping on the wooden ties between the polished rails.

He had been on the track a while when the sky began to lighten behind him. The sun was well risen when the track bent into the mouth of a cave. Xue Bao thought of sleeping in there, but he knew without being able to say it that it was not a good place. Words grew harder; but he sensed more. He looked for a different resting place and saw a granite block thrust out from the canyon wall, several feet above the cave entrance. Climbing to it, he found a flat space and sat with his arms wrapped around his knees. Then he lay down on the hard surface, curled his body, and slept.

Xue Bao dreamed of a big blue-sheep ewe in the half-light at the onset of dawn, of effortless bounding down scree, claws parting hair and sinking into hide, pulling the ewe off her hooves, rolling and holding. Xue Bao was dreaming when a sound he had heard before came into his sleep, and he opened his eyes and lost all memory of the dream.

From the angle of the sun trying to sear through the gray-yellow cataract over the sky, Xue Bao saw it was midday. The awakening sound was the shriek he had heard the last time he was in the canyon. Spying over the granite edge, he saw the black-green thing with yellow-striped flanks, trudging up the trail toward the cave, exhaling smoke.

There was a word for this thing; and for a moment, in his head, Xue Bao was back in a building with many people droning in all directions, searching for the word that eluded him. His sense was, though, that he should travel on this thing into the cave.

The thing did not move fast as it slid into the opening, black smoke pluming behind and filling the air around Xue Bao. He let it slink much of its length inside, then he stood and went to the edge of the granite. Xue Bao could not see through the smoke, but he knew the thing lay beneath it. He sprang, arms and legs spanned.

Plunging through the smoke, Xue Bao tucked and landed on feet and hands, flattening himself at once. Xue Bao lay on the thing's carapace without moving as it crawled into the stone mouth, and in a moment he was in a smoke-filled place of rumbling choking darkness.

Xue Bao squirmed his body around to face the direction he traveled. The ceiling of the cave was close, so he did not lift his head. He squeezed his eyes tight to keep out the sooty smoke and hot cinders. The rumbling was all around, rolling off the enveloping rock. Then it was gone, and there was just a clacking and the sound of the wind and the smell of cleaner air. Xue Bao slit open his eyes and looked ahead.

The segmented back of the thing extended hundreds of feet ahead, the black smoke rising high into the air and blowing back over him. The shell-back Xue Bao lay on rocked as it moved, soothing him so that he drowsed as he was borne to higher country.

It was a slow climb, and not until late in the day did the winding canyons give over to level treeless plains. The speed rose and the clacking quickened and air rushed over Xue Bao, the tear in his sleeve fluttering. The air turned colder and carried a new scent, a distant trace of a mountain. He clamped his hand onto the fur hide and lifted his head. He saw mud-brick houses and land in plotted shapes, but no one in the fields or walking toward the houses as the sun set.

At dark the thing gave a short bellow and slowed. An arrow of small blue lights pointed ahead, the lights separating and growing larger and taller as the thing drew near. The thing passed over a dry wash and crawled between two files of lampposts holding the blue lights. With a loud release of steam, the thing came to a halt.

Xue Bao raised his head. To the left was a long raised flat ledge of stone with long sitting places set on it and behind it an earthen-colored building with a red-tiled roof and many square openings with lights in them. No one was on the ledge or sitting places or in the building. Xue Bao slid to the right and looked up and down the length of the thing. Swinging his feet over, he took a breath, kicked out, and dropped from its right flank.

His boots spraying gravel when he landed, Xue Bao kept low, waiting, his bandaged hand brushing the metal-and-horn holder on his belt. He listened, but the only sound was a regular chuffing from the thing. He rose.

Through thin sheets of ice along its flank above the yellow band, Xue Bao looked into the thing and saw rows of sitting places, all empty. Xue Bao ducked his head and trotted toward the rear.

Xue Bao came to the wash the black-green thing had passed over as it was drawing to a halt, and dropped into it. Keeping low, he came to an opening that passed beneath the trail the thing traveled on; and he went under the trail and jogged up the wash.

The wash's worn banks ran by mud-brick houses. Some of the houses had lights, but no sounds came from them. After several miles Xue Bao saw a trail passing along the wash, and he climbed to it. The trail was made of broad black unbroken stone that Xue Bao knew, but no longer had any word for. He looked up and down it. Seeing no lights, he began to walk, heading uphill.

In the darkness no lights or moving things came from either direction on the trail. Xue Bao passed dusty fields and soundless mud-brick buildings, without even the barking from a herdsman's dog that should have caught his scent. The moon was not yet up; and it was hard to see the rising of the land; but he could feel it in his legs, telling him that the high plateau lay ahead, and beyond it the mountain.

Late in the night the trail passed beneath a gate with dragons carved in wood at its top. In the daylight he would have been able to distinguish the red and gold they were painted in. Xue Bao knew he had passed through this dragon gate before and sniffed to see if he had marked it with his scent, smelling nothing of himself. Here the black stone gave way to packed dirt.

Xue Bao followed the trail between two rows of one-story buildings. Tonight there was no scent of scorching meat or the sight of a floppy-eared pig, nor any squeals. Beyond the buildings the trail curved, and he followed it until he came to the bottom of the steep ravine filled with snow. Xue Bao climbed.

He could not move over the top of the snow but broke the crust and sank to the tops of the shiny black skin that covered his hind paws. It was near dawn when he climbed out of the ravine into a pass, able to look out on the plateau and feel again the cold west wind.

Against the skyline he saw a tall pole set in a pile of rocks, ropes tethering it, hundreds of frayed many-colored gossamer cloths, some with figures on them, flapping from the pole and the ropes. The wind made Xue Bao want to go on, but his nightlong's walking and hunger had taken his strength. He lay down at its base, wrapped in an inside-out hide that was not as warm as his spotted fur, the hide on his head pulled down over his eyes.

Waking late in the day, Xue Bao pushed the hide back on his head and looked toward where the mountain should be in the distance. The sky was not the gray-yellow murk of the place of buildings, streets, and people, now fading from his mind. It was the dust-filled red-tinted pearl color he knew from the mountain, in the air the smell of rock and snow. He scraped the ground and made urine, scuffing the soil back over it, then wrapped himself up in his hide and began walking again.

Xue Bao's head burred with hunger, like bees hunting nectar in white flowers in green summer grass. His stomach was so long without food, it no longer ached. He did not let his steps slow, though, as he crossed the sandy soil of the plateau and patches of windrowed snow. Night came, and in the middle of it he passed by a herd of white-blazed tame yaks bedded on the plateau. They stood and circled their calves until he was far away.

As dawn filled the sky at his back, Xue Bao saw something ahead on the empty plateau. It was not the mountain but an outcrop of weathered sandstone. The sides were steep, but there were enough cracks in the soft crumbling stone that he was able to climb to its flat top. Standing there, he looked around and found a place clean of the white droppings of griffons and eagles. He lay down on his side and pulled the hide low on his head, and the great hide coat, with the fur on the wrong side, tight around him. He drew his arms up into the too-long sleeves and crossed them on his chest, then closed his eyes.

Xue Bao slept through the day and into the night. His eyes moved behind their lids, and his limbs swiped at the sandy rock while his lungs filled with the smells of the plateau and the air off the mountain, carried to him by the west wind that came at winter's end.

ACROSS THE PLATEAU a section of light fell across the ground as a heavy-lidded herdsman opened a door of thick wool felt in the wall of a round tent. He remembered starting his ride home from singing to the music of a lute, smoking tobacco, and drinking barley wine in the tent of his uncle; but then he must have slept and let the pony find the way. The pony was skittish as he unsaddled and hobbled and turned it out to graze. Now, steadying himself at the door, he saw fragments of a mystifying dream at the boundary of recall, as something made him lower his hand toward the dagger sheath on his belt.

Xue Bao opened jade eyes as a slender bow of shadow slid off the face of the full moon at dawn. He woke from emptiness and lay on his side, legs extended, looking into the sinking pale-orange orb. Moving his head, he saw that he was on a flat tower of sandstone on a treeless wind-scoured plateau.

Flexing his toes and extending his claws, Xue Bao got to his four large round furred paws. He swayed his back and stretched his body, yawned, touched his long ivory-yellow fangs with his rasped tongue. He circled the top of the tower, looking.

The wind lay down, and Xue Bao saw out to the horizon. Snow sparkled in the last of the moonlight like the shards of a shattered looking glass, the mountain lying beneath. Padding in slow strides to the edge of the tower, he sought a way down. Pausing, he looked behind. His thick furred tail hung low, brushing the ground. He twitched its tip. His long whiskers bristled. He made two jumps down the face of the tower and landed on the sandy ground of the plateau and began walking toward the mountain where, as his hunger directed him, he must hunt.

At daybreak Xue Bao saw a single tan-and-white gazelle buck far off on the flat of the plateau. The buck's ribbed horns described black reverse curves, and it stretched up its neck and head as it watched him. Xue Bao only looked at the gazelle once, seeing it diluted in the morning shimmer, then looked straight ahead as he walked on to the mountain.

Xue Bao reached the foothills at the end of the morning and went on in the daylight, ascending canyons and draws, wearied by hunger but refusing to stop because he might not keep going. The ground rose faster but felt more familiar than the level land below. It was almost evening when he saw blue sheep.

The small band floated in the mirrored haze across a rocky bowl. Xue Bao used the rocks and scattered clumps of low alpine plants to hide as he stalked, pressed to the ground. His hunger made him break from cover too soon, the dozen animals disappearing over the rim of the bowl a hundred feet ahead of him, racing down the rocks on the other side where Xue Bao could not catch them.

The failed chase cost him strength, but he went on. Each step was like lifting an ever-increasing weight, but by night he was far up in the heart of the mountain again. Here he had a last chance to hunt.

When Xue Bao could not climb any higher, he lay on a ledge on a cliff above a saddle. In the light of the moon he could see three ridges out. A buzzing like tiger-headed hornets filled his brain. He had to catch and kill the next blue sheep in one bound because he would not be able to chase it beyond that. If a sheep came, he could not miss. If a sheep came.

Having no more words or thoughts, Xue Bao lay on the mountain. Through his skin beneath the amber-gray fur that clung to him like living fog, he absorbed it. The mountain was in the muscles at the base of his tail, in his chest inside the laddered ribs, and in that bright place behind his jade eyes, the pupils wide now, drawing in all the light, searching for any movement on the ridges. Lying on the ledge, he stored his strength for one last chase. There could be only one; but if it failed, or if blue sheep did not come, he would be on the mountain and nowhere else. That was enough.

Xue Bao tried watching all night but could not keep awake. Early the next morning he opened his eyes to see a herd of blue sheep feeding up the slope in slow, staggered bands, kicking through snow, then grazing out onto the short dry stubble of snow-free sparse mountain grass covering the saddle. Xue Bao felt the strength for one leap, one burst to grab and hold. The sheep spread out over the saddle, the older ones feeding at a distance from the cliff. A few lambs and young rams and ewes strayed beneath him.

With so much weight lost, it was easy for Xue Bao to turn around on the narrow ledge within the length of his own body without loosening a rock or being seen by the sheep below. Now he faced down, along the incline of the ledge, concealed within the spotted fur of his hide.

Xue Bao watched a young ewe. He felt the movements that must be made. They coiled in his flesh, the toes of his forepaws trembling. There was a narrowing of his sight that made him see one blue sheep alone out of the herd. All the others were excluded from his vision. He saw only this single ewe, this one web of senses and synapses that must not detect him before he had caught it in his claws.

His head was buoyant yet seemed impossible to support. Xue Bao's eyes wanted to close, but he would not take them off the ewe. She was coming to the place where his slanting ledge met the saddle. Xue Bao's jaw was slack as he panted shallow breaths. From his lower lip spun a silver thread of saliva, swaying from the fur of his chin. The sheep's back was to him as she fed to where the ledge came to the saddle.

In a bound five times the length of his body Xue

Bao leaped from the ledge. At the last second the ewe's head snapped up. She broke into a run, the rest of her band, and then the whole herd, flying from her like the scatterings of a dandelion from a puff of wind. When he touched the saddle, Xue Bao's momentum carried him to her in one pounce, the other blue sheep rushing over the saddle. Catching her by the flanks with his claws, he pulled himself onto her and rolled beneath, setting his fangs into her windpipe and clamping it shut as they both rolled over together.

Xue Bao lay on the sheep, his jaws still on her throat, his large paws pressing down, claws fixed in her. He felt her kicking legs weaken, then felt her die. He waited a minute, two minutes more, then released his bite. He lay beside her for some time, motionless and silent. At last he moved to the sheep's rump and with an almost reluctant bite began to open her hide with his cutting side teeth. At first he tried to eat slow; but his hunger made him rush, and his stomach was not ready for so much blood-filled meat. He had to stop and cough out what he had eaten. He ate slower, then.

The pounds of meat Xue Bao ate made him thirsty. He walked off the saddle, looking back at the carcass several times, and down the slope on the snow. Near the bottom, the slope fell into a rock wash. In the wash a lamb, separated from the band when it fled, dashed back and forth, bleating, until it saw Xue Bao. Then it turned and ran as he watched it.

He found a pool of milky meltwater dammed by tumbled rocks and lapped until the water and the sheep meat felt heavy in his belly. Xue Bao wanted sleep, but he climbed back up the slope.

Scavenger birds sailed across the sky. When Xue Bao came to the carcass, he took it by the neck with his teeth and dragged it backward to the base of the cliff he had sprung from and pulled loose rocks over it with his front paws. Then he found a place above it where he could curl into the cliff and sleep.

Xue Bao fed on the ewe for four days. When there was no more wild meat but only bones and hide and hooves left, he went on. Where there was fissured rock Xue Bao's toughened pads carried him without hurt, and the fur of his paws let him cross banks of crusted drifts. A white snowcock burst upward in a tantrum of wings. On one field of snow Xue Bao cut melted-out wolf tracks, but they were old and fading. He climbed far into the mountain, then began to circle, the shape of his body and long tail hidden behind the ridgelines.

Light left the sky. High on the slopes Xue Bao came to a cave and found his own scent. The moonrise through the opening would wake him when it was time to hunt again. The wind lay down and he lay in the mouth of the cave in the empty stillness, licking the fur on his chest and the backs of his paws and rubbing them over his short scarred muzzle. Then

Xue Bao went into the cave and circled, turning in the length of his body, lowering himself onto his belly. He wrapped his thick tail around his muzzle.

He listened. From far below through the windless air came a herdsman's dog's gong-like bark. Then Xue Bao lifted his head for a moment at the sustained note of an echoing call. Much farther away, far, far below, a horn-handled dagger rested silent in bamboo leaf fall. When the moon rose in the clear sky, its bone-white light would show across Xue Bao's forepaw a healing, clean-edged wound, the blood dried some time ago.

Now Xue Bao closed his eyes. Tonight there would be no dream, because this was not a place of dreams or of shadows that were not made by the sun or moon. This was Bountiful Black Mountain, ancient and rounded by wind and snow and time. Here Xue Bao could sleep dreamless, yet listening on as he slept. Always listening.

雪豹

ACKNOWLEDGMENTS

FOURTEEN YEARS AGO NOW, on a March afternoon in 1998, I stood at the window in a rear room of a hotel 6,500 miles away, looking out through the open curtains over the rough gray roofs and streets and alleys of Xining, an old desert city (old by Western if not Chinese standards) that was once a trading center for camel caravans traveling the Northern Silk Road; and a tale began to spin. I had descended from the dust-swirled Tibetan-Qinghai Plateau and the mountains in which lay the source of the Yellow River (accompanied on the journey by my late friend and mentor Roy Cooper and my extant good friend Carey Caruso), where I rode ponies to 16,000 feet, visited a Buddhist *dzong*, slept by the heat of a sheep-dung stove under the

Dharmachakra wooden crown of a ger, saw blue sheep and Tibetan gazelle, met a robed giant, and did not see a snow leopard, as perhaps it should be—though if a snow leopard saw me, I cannot say. The true inception of the story, though, began years before with a single image, the photo of an Afghan girl on the cover of a magazine, staring out with feral, maybe wild, green eyes. In those eyes I thought I glimpsed the spark of the relict animal that dwells in us all.

Until I went to China, though, I had not found the story in which to write about that spark; and then from out of those mountains I had just departed, I thought of pursuit and flight and consciousness, the last a mystery which has intrigued me since my reading of Julian Jaynes's *The Origin of Consciousness in the Breakdown of the Bicameral Mind* some thirty years ago. Weary from days of travel, I nonetheless made myself turn from the window and put down an outline in a college-ruled composition book, believing I hadn't the privilege of squandering an idea. And returning home, I began to write.

I might wish to represent that this started out as a sprawling canvas that was scraped down and distilled into pure substance by dint of the strictest critical judgment, but the truth is that it was always a rather slender story in which I wrote all I had to say. Some to whom I ventured to show it liked it from the outset. Stephen J. Bodio, of course (I think Steve will appreciate the sincerity of that "of course"), praised it following a first reading. Then there was the late Robert F. Jones who enthusiastically brainstormed ways of ushering it into print, concerned from a marketing standpoint about its brevity while detecting affinities, somehow, with the work of Michel Houellebecq, whose writing regrettably I have yet to read. My long-time non-fiction editor Jay Cassell made a valiant, broken-field run with the book. Russell Chatham came close to publishing it through his Clark City Press many years ago; but fate, or providence, intervened, no doubt to the betterment of the writing, if I may suggest. So I continued revising, producing a new version practically perennially, having copies run off at the UPS store, mailing unsolicited submissions to scores of publishing houses to no other avail than the return of the manuscript with a form letter and the forlorn stain of a coffee ring on the title page. Or sometimes no return at all.

During early days the poet Sam Western read a draft and said, no, not right, not yet, and was, again of course, correct. Certain natural-history frolics of mine were open to question, as when at a reading from the work in Billings, Doug Peacock diplomatically sniffed that he had never thought of dholes meeting up with snow leopards (which now, in this version of the book, they happily do not).

I carried the manuscript with me, searching for a geographic cure. I spent a late-spring month isolated in a house provided by Sharon Cornthwaite in piney Story, Wyoming, retyping the manuscript on a manual Olivetti, probing for an elusive element of whose existence serious doubts were rising. It accompanied me to Buenos Aires in what was, yes, a form of pilgrimage or hajj to the place of birth of the creator of "Tlön, Uqbar, Orbis Tertius." But even with all that, the tale never achieved that, truly, *je nais se quoi*. And then back home, one more revision seemed to have arrived, unbidden, at the place where it ought to be, or at least as high as my reach extended.

By various curious turns, this is the story Allen Jones, publisher of Bangtail Press, saw and, may God shelter him in His palm, thought enough of to want to grant his imprint. After which he pointed out so very many solecisms which in near invincible ignorance I'd failed to recognize, even after such a long span of time and so much strenuous effort.

In a little while others became involved in the enterprise, such as the artist Joel Ostlind (who as we discussed ideas for illustrations unaccountably produced a relatively obscure anthology of *Black Mask* stories that I myself owned), the estimable photographer Adam Jahiel (tasked with making *some*thing out of the sow's ear that is the author's image), and Ted Kerasote, whose close reading and input on the tale have been invaluable. And Steven Stathatos, Esquire, who cast a reasonably forensic eye over certain written agreements, proving, in a paraphrase of Dr. Hunter S. Thompson's three-hundred-pound Samoan attorney, that even a leopard-man is entitled to legal counsel.

Finally, but never least, there are my son Bryan, who literally grew up during the writing, and more so rewriting, of this story, and my wife Elaine, who has lived through the vicissitudes of this long, strange trip without failing to maintain her love for me, while now I can only offer mine to her, once more.

Adam Jahiel

An award-winning professional writer for more than thirty-five years, **Tom McIntyre** has authored thousands of magazine articles and television scripts, and is the author of such critically-acclaimed books as *Days Afield*, *Dreaming the Lion*, and *Seasons & Days*. Born and raised in California, he moved to northern Wyoming almost twenty years ago with his wife, Elaine, and son, Bryan. *The Snow Leopard's Tale* is his first novel.

CPSIA information can be obtained at www.ICGtesting.com
Printed in the USA
LVOW13s1919170713

343352LV00015B/1317/P